Hales 908

For Bettye
from Doug,

with affectionate
wishes —

The

DANCER

and the

DANCE

One Man's Chronicle   1938–2001

YALE   LAWRENCE   DUKE   QUESTAR

The Individual
The Community
The Educated Life

BY DOUGLAS M. KNIGHT

Separate Star

IN MEMORY

Maynard Mack
William Clyde DeVane

Stern Mentors   Loving Friends

Many friends have contributed their time and talent to the making of this book. Among them I particularly wish to thank Meredith Bergmann, Blythe Boquist, Eleanor Elliott, Elizabeth Forter, William Griffiths, Bridget Jones, John McCardell, Charles Muscatine, Steven Samuelson, Frederick Starr and Richard Warch. My special gratitude must go to my publisher, Michael Bergmann, and my Associate Rebekah Wade. Without them there would be no book.

TABLE OF CONTENTS

INTRODUCTION

A shilling life will give you all the facts, but here I have something else in mind. My life, with its multiple careers and wide-ranging experience, has led me to ask what useful sense I can make of it: how does one reconcile university teaching and scholarship, heavy academic administrative work for nearly twenty years, equally heavy involvement in a unique optical company for almost thirty and decades of writing poetry? Do the pieces go together in a coherent, informative way? My conviction that they do has emerged clearly as I consider the varied events of my life.

The last sixty years have been a time of remarkable change in higher education. It was my good fortune to be in the last class to finish Yale before the Second World War. There I enjoyed the best of a great genteel tradition. I was lured at an early age into university administration and forced out of it at the end of the tumultuous 60s. My diverse experiences over the following decades have invariably involved some form of educational activity—much of it outside the academy. As I have explored them I have realized that their real value lies not in myself but in those educational and social events where I played some small part.

It is the unique nature of a memoir to confront reality, but to be highly selective about it. A memoir makes constant judgments about society and yet is bound to the life of its writer. It is not a comprehensive historical account of events but an illumination of those experiences that give body to a life. It has a major text—the action—and an equally important subtext that grows from the action but plays against it both as commentary and as motivation for the action still to come. I hope to bring to life this duality of action and inference that is, indeed, at the heart of all enduring experience. Neither novel nor biography, a memoir shares its character with both. In that sharing an intimate texture of life emerges—must emerge—but it is wedded to a growing separation between the immediate narrative actions and the trajectory they assume. That arrow of time has not only a path but also a purpose: it reveals the meaning of those myriad decisions which much of the time seem unrelated and without any large implied meaning.

In counterpoint to my personal experience, for example, we have the great sixty year drama of American education itself, revealing its remarkable pattern of change and growth as our culture shifts from the euphoria of the 50s to the unforeseen turbulence of the 60s and the tightening both of structure and management which took place in the 70s, to be succeeded in turn by a steadily increasing dispersion of educational means and purposes in the 80s and 90s. (Surprisingly, this emergent pattern is evident even in the worst aspects of the period.) This dynamism has resulted in the exuberant diversity of education that we find at the end of the past century and the beginning of our new millennium. Contention in the formal academy will be matched by the larger energy of myriad new ventures and their ability to adapt to the whole country's felt need—a far cry indeed from the minority privileges of higher education sixty years earlier. Both the text and the subtext of this book relate intimately to the development of these patterns in higher education.

There are two distinct periods of my experience. The first, from 1938 to 1969, takes the logical, though accelerated, shape of an academic career, a career that ended abruptly, to my great regret, at the midpoint of my life. The sequel has been a thirty-year journey through entirely new country. That journey has led to a radical extension of my views of education as an active—indeed central—part of our culture. I am privileged to have had a new career quite beyond anything I could have imagined, and it redefined for me the central meaning of the educated life. That discovery defines the second major focus of this book with its emphasis on that duality which embodies the central purpose of liberal learning—to live simultaneously the action and the perceived significance of it. This dual activity is a dance with two dancers—the dancer of the action and his twin who shapes the critical and creative effort that sustains the action. We cannot know the direction and value of our action without this constant partner who brings a sympathetic but critical and indeed tutorial eye to bear on each step we take. The underlying order of this book, of my life, emerges as a story within a story—an apologia for a certain way of living based on the great traditions of liberal learning. This unity of direction comes from an understanding of the action, of the critical judgments and emerging convictions that lend it substance and direction. The great physicist Richard Feynman said that underlying his life's work, and driving it constantly, was the pleasure of finding things out. I would say the same of my own life, and therefore of this book. It is an attempt to find out through my active life what the world of our personal and yet communal existence is about—partial and limited as the result must be.

The title of this memoir comes from the concluding lines of Yeats's poem, *Among School Children*. This image, which Yeats develops brilliantly in several poems, is a testimony to pattern in life and, beyond that, a particular sense of it with a complex relevance to our common experience. Yeats captures the creating function of our actions; they build a sustained pattern for experience beyond their individual and partial nature. More deeply, perception and the expression of that perception become one. We do not know what we understand until we articulate it; then our articulation becomes the meaning. Yeats thus describes all creating activity, which must fuse the creator and the creation, whether it be the making of a poem or a career. The "action" creates the meaning of the event or the person; it seems to me the right image for this book, which is concerned equally with the experience of one person and the large substance of his encounters. The latter is objective to him and at the same time only seen as he manages to see it. This is a book of myself and of much that I have seen and tried to influence in the varied worlds of education, which, in some bizarre forms indeed, have been the substance of my life.

A word about myself...Although I have

chosen for this book the part of my life that began with my freshman year in college, certain aspects of my boyhood may suggest my later interests. I am an only child. My father was injured in France during World War I, and his additional exposure to mustard gas made him an ideal pneumonia victim. After his death (when I was five) I spent the next five years being encouraged and spoiled by my mother, my aunt and my grandmother. My mother tried valiantly to support us through her teaching, but the demands of my grandparents constantly interrupted this pattern. As a result we moved several times a year, and by the time I entered junior high school I had been in thirteen different elementary schools—and each time was the victim of the craze for intelligence tests, as we called them.

Consequently I was pushed ahead, missing much that I should have learned—the transition from arithmetic to mathematics, for example. Fortunately I matured physically very early, so that I was not a freak in class when I entered seventh grade at the age of ten. Junior high school was, blessedly, all in one place: Boston in the depth of the depression. A footnote on geography: I lived in Boston as a small boy—was born in Cambridge—and returned there in 1930 for orthodontic work. My mother's work for the government took me to Washington at three different times, but my strong center in this scattered life was my grandfather's working farm in Old Lyme, one of the wealthiest towns in the country. Here he employed his great skill with landscaping and plant breeding. Both at that time and later my mother and I were helped financially by a wonderfully generous friend who made it possible for my crooked teeth to be put in some order, and also suggested that I go to a school to which her brother-in-law, Edward Harkness, had just made a major gift for the support of small-class teaching. This was Exeter; I entered the upper middle class as a frightened fourteen-year-old, was overwhelmed for two or three months and was hopelessly in love with the place by the time the Christmas holiday came. Indeed I found that Washington had no magic for me, and two days after Christmas I told my mother that I had work to do, packed my suitcase and headed back. I will never forget the snowy evening of the trip north of Boston; the old Boston and Maine cars had open vestibules, and the brakeman ran through the train at every stop to tighten the brakes by hand.

I remember equally the startled look on my housemaster's face when he answered my knock. He and his wife were stymied for only a moment; they took me in and must somehow have fed me for a week until classes began. I remember the freedom of the library; it gave me a wonderful center for my life that I had first encountered at the library in Old Lyme.

Exeter gave me exactly what I needed—extreme expectations, great variety, the new seminar system supported by Mr. Harkness' gift, and that sense of intellectual community that I had never experienced before. After graduating I planned to stay on for an extra year—I was still fifteen—but a bout of pneumonia demanded that I leave the New Hampshire climate and go south to college for the winter and spring. That experience was an innocent but intoxicating glimpse of girls, convertibles, and general *laissez faire*. I left as virginal as I arrived, but with a vivid sense that there was a new world to be explored. In retrospect I realize that it was just as well I had only four months of Babylon although the taste on the tongue was wonderful. To move from Rollins College to Yale was a shock of another kind: a thousand classmates, a preeminent university, and all the apprehensive delight of stepping into a major new world.

For the next fifteen years I savored this new world, as an undergraduate, as a graduate student and finally as a young teacher. I left it to serve for ten years as President of Lawrence University, then for more than six years as President of Duke University where my clearly delineated academic career ended abruptly. There followed years—dark years—of finding a new way in life. These years were a journey that took me to many places, including Iran for prolonged periods. This journey eventually ended with my entering (quite unpredictably) a wonderful and exciting world revolving around the Questar Corporation, a small but extremely fine maker of quality telescopes and other optical instruments. Throughout my post academic life I have remained intimately engaged in various educational interests including my service as Chairman of the Board of the Woodrow Wilson Fellowship Foundation.

A ROOM WITH A VIEW*

Behind sweet ramparts
Of well-being, we paraded
Our toys, showed them with style,
Even invited neighbors in
To push the buttons, change the dials.
In that fat time there seemed no room
In the great house for private matters.
They shrank, to fit
The small, left-over spaces. It was
A time for Babel, and the seductions
Of our soft sensuous empires.

But once the walls were down,
There was space, a room left
From the ruin: plain,
No trophy cases, no lacquer. But
There is light through great windows.
The landscape has teasing distances—
No foregrounds manicured, no rigid borders.
But a new music for my ears.
I had not known how it might be
Without the guile and clutter—a richness
Of memory but a child's directness.
And a passion to embrace
The infinite depth of now, its
Bounty beyond all reason,
Its refutation of age.

* *All poems are by the author.*

CHAPTER ONE:
The Voices of Our Culture
1990–2001

Our present decade, which bridges two
centuries, is one of such turmoil and dissent in community
life—and therefore in education—that it must be our first
focus of concern. The last decades of the twentieth century
created a more diverse educational community than has existed
in any culture before now. My personal experience over the
span of six decades may be useful in evoking this present in its
conflicting variety and offer some explanation of *why* we are
as we are.

As we try to understand our decade in its rapid and conflicting motion we must admit that no one can grasp it properly. It is
a time of amazing social interaction and equal isolation; the fields
of social force grow enormous while the yearning for personal
identity also grows rapidly and insistently. Henry Adams saw this
same profound tension a century ago; we have changed the technology but not the conflict. We may consider this decade's dual

history using Plato's metaphor for our difficult and uncertain apprehension of reality: the images we think we see, the paradigms of our thought, are only flickering images on a wall; they reflect partially and inaccurately the truth of things. That warning is essential when we try to describe realities which are in rapid process but which also form our immediate context and the field of our activity. It does seem, however, that five major concerns are shaping the pattern of our society at the moment. Some have been gathering strength for years; some are recent, but none can be set aside. They are the necessary bases for active education and all thoughtful life in the years just ahead.

The end of the Cold War brought a euphoria that was deserved but dangerous. There was such yearning to see one great threat removed that the revelation of other major world problems came as a shock. As long as there were two major antagonists they imposed a rough discipline on other conflicts. With the end of the Soviet Empire a swarm of these broke out, both between countries and within them. The examples are everywhere, and they impose terrible burdens on innocent populations, always the chief victims of public violence. One major result has been the destabilizing and forced migration of millions of people; they in turn have the power to disrupt the societies around them. The urgent necessity to reestablish and maintain order worldwide gives a whole new dimension to our own society, and thus to the new purposes of education. We must shape patterns of society that make room equally for local and global relationships. We have spoken of this tension in the past at an abstract level; now it is urgent and immediate.

One immediate driving force behind our social urgency springs from the cluster of technical developments that has forced us into intimacy in our social and political relationships. Our fearful military competence is matched by instant communication systems that allow us to transfer money or gossip, salvation or destruction with equal ease. Having this great gift we are often its victims. We learn partial truth and take no time to qualify it; our power to generate information grows exponentially, but we lack the time or the means to shape it into knowledge and judgment. We were promised simplification through these great technical advances, and lives with ample leisure. As we all know, we work harder than ever, and often it takes two of us to earn one adequate living for our families. Our technologies are costly, it seems, and not comfortably in our control. They have changed the pace of life, but they have done less to improve its quality. I certainly do not wish to be thought a Luddite or a nostalgic dreamer; I would not break the machines if I could, but I would gladly see us as their masters rather than their servants or their naive and uncritical dupes. In Eliot's great metaphor, we must find again the still point of the turning world so that we have a standard of judgment for interpreting it. I am looking for an antidote to the alluring poison of systems, networks, strategies which are sold to us as somehow excellent in themselves. Perhaps I ask that these grand systems of communication find something more substantial to communicate than their self-declared excellence.

In contrast to these problematic powers of our technical world stands the equally formidable emergence of women as in many new ways the major shaping force of our society. They have created nothing less than a fundamental shift in our social structure. This has not been easy, and its inner meaning has been obscured by some gaudy deviations of the formal feminist movement—essential as the movement itself has been in achieving a larger sense of the new and 'equal' place of women. That devilish word *equal* is still the problem, of course; it has brought with it a delusive hope that gender distinctions can also be erased. As a result, the greatest gains of the new role of women are diminished and even denigrated. I have had the privilege of working with very able women all my life; they have brought to our common efforts not only their great talents but a different mode of using them, which is often a corrective to masculine ego compulsions. This reality is still argued, but the strength that women bring to our society is of their own kind; they have not learned to be like men but to be confidently and powerfully themselves. As we look at the forces shaping education, this may well be the most important.

Women may be the most powerful group, but the fastest growing is, of course, the mature and elderly part of society. Its members owe their shaping power in education, as everywhere else, to their experience, their often-proved competence, and their financial stability. They are the group which defines the new market for education in its broadest sense. By demonstrating so forcefully that education never ends, they set a pattern for their juniors—and not only because they use highly creative means of educating themselves, but because they have done so much to break the restrictions which used to stereotype our later years. They are the leaven in society; they have more freedom than others, they are less bound by convention, and many are prime examples of what it means to be actively educated. In this way their example, like that of women, can be an agent of change in our understanding of education in action.

I am glorifying my own age group, but I see that they stand a better chance of looking at the essential elements of good life and good society than any of the younger groups. They are beyond fads and trendiness, and with better health at seventy (for example) than any previous generation they can be a determining force for the future because they still *have* a future to match and fulfill their past. And they have one remarkable attribute beyond these others; they are philanthropic, often creatively so. They can afford to take positive pleasure in their generosity, particularly in their use of some of the new ways of giving. The result, of course, is that they stir and stimulate generosity in others—an ideal contribution to the health of educational institutions and to society at large.

The importance of these current realities and emerging groups in society leads inevitably to one aspect of our life today that underlies all the others in shaping and defining our concerns—both social and individual. A ground base of spiritual ferment colors the self-image and conflicted purpose of whole societies today. In Israel we see it as the conflict between the orthodox Rabbinate and the rest of Israeli culture. In Iran it has been a twenty-year conflict between the orthodox Mullahs and the more tolerant, less militant Iranian society (reflecting in turn a far longer schism between clerical and secular beliefs). In our country of 260 million people the diversities of belief are enormous; what makes them so significant is that they reflect in all their variety a deep concern for spiritual definitions and practices. Despite the militancy of the Christian Coalition and others of like mind, we do not as a culture accept aggressive attempts to take doctrinaire control of our spiritual and political lives. We respect the *fact* of those spiritual lives, however, and equally the wild diversity that a culture as vibrant as ours seems to engender. Our multiculturalism has a good deal to do with this flexibility; as a result I suspect that much of the resistance to recent immigration comes from the same groups that are asserting the claims of a restrictive religious orthodoxy most vigorously. They fear the further increase in diversity which new citizens bring.

But why are these multiple spiritual concerns so important? Because they suggest a willingness to examine fundamental thought and conviction—which is the chief function of all liberated education. Equally, as I see the college and university worlds today, these spiritual concerns are the—often unacknowledged—bases for the conflicts of purpose and standard which mark formal education so strongly at the moment.

The broader educational scene includes all five of these urgent realities. Taken together they create the limit conditions through which we can give some order to the 'mighty maze' of institutions, programs and ideologies which *are* American education and society at the present time. The context for these major elements of society (its laminates if you will) is the daily reality within which we live, the cluster of limit conditions that we inhabit. Its three chief elements shape our daily lives but also often determine the kinds of education we find essential.

First and most striking is the cultural world-order, which gives us our styles of food, architecture, music and art. One country may dominate; music in America might seem an obvious example, but it would not exist without Africa and Brazil. We take a world cuisine completely for granted, and we have almost a compulsion toward clothing that uses material and styling from what used to be the most exotic corners of the earth. Our architects build in Sydney, Tokyo or Burgos.

This cultural diffusion is equally at home in the most eclectic spirituality and the loudest, most cult-oriented aspects of pop culture. And one of its great characteristics is the ease with which we move from the superficial to the profound—and back again. Our 'personalities' last a week of overexposure, while our yearnings of the heart can reach into the culture of the ages for their imagery. We are not trivial, but we often make a crazy pattern from our trivialities.

We move in a world of cultural paradoxes, and we find ourselves equally out of harmony when we look at our political/governmental/military world, which now manages to fracture all easy ideas of order. At the end of WWII we based our strong support of the United Nations on a hope of world discipline that could contain our dark taste for violence. We managed it—barely—in the relationship of the superpowers, but with two unpredicted results. First, while we continue to inch toward world-order we are increasingly disenchanted with nation-states. That great European invention is now under constant threat from its own sub-national ethnic and political structures. Second, while we have avoided the Armageddon war we face a constant assault on civil society from a barrage of small wars—at least forty of them at any given time. Their origins are many, but all of them involve some form of deep discontent with the structures of government, the limited rights of citizens, or the chaos of religious aggression in myriad forms. Our hopes are still those we described for ourselves fifty years ago, but the scale and complexity of events has overwhelmed us. We can handle intellectually the idea of a world society, but emotionally we are gratified only by the small units where we can find ourselves fully alive. And the demon of terrorism springs from this last reality; it is the idea of small community turned inside out, the worst of paradoxes—great violence sustained by tiny cell groups.

The economic complexities that have unfolded in the last fifty years also build their order from a cluster of paradoxes. The wealthiest large nation demands of its successful citizens long hours, brief vacations and a dual income in order to make full use of its consumer economy. The leisure society predicted in 1950 is as chimerical as the paperless offices promised by the computer salesman. Meanwhile on an international scale everyone has become his neighbor's keeper, and an ailment in Djarkata is chills and fever on Wall Street. English is fast becoming the international language of business, but the ease of communication about business matters does little by itself to resolve complex economic questions. The reason for this ice jam is the greatest paradox of all. We have astonishing amounts of economic information available on a minute by minute basis, but our great decisions—and indecisions—are matters of passions rather than equations. The issues affecting society are most often governed by money; yet who would claim to make rational sense out of the stock market? Common sense suggests that a healthy society needs some balance of income across the spectrum from rich to poor; yet with us the disparity continues to grow.

The cumulative effect of these three major vectors of our world—cultural, political and economic—is striking and bewildering. The urgencies that inhabit all three create for us a world society of conflict, diversity, kaleidoscopic change, and above all *energy*. We have myriad questions to resolve, while unlike our clarity and consensus in the last period of great urgency and growth just after WWII we are now unsure of the standards and norms to use in resolving our policy issues. We have creative force to spare, while we are not sure how to use it. And as we turn to questions of educational order at the present time, we see it responding in remarkable ways to the urgency of these social and individual needs—and to their confusions.

Much that is now available to us in the American community was beyond thought sixty years ago. The university world that I entered in 1938 was the major path to education beyond secondary school; the great public and private universities carried the primary burden of that 15% of high school graduates who continued their education. (There was also of course a second tier of public and private universities—in the great cities, for the most part.) States like New Jersey and Massachusetts did not have strong public institutions, so that their students were either 'exported,' enrolled in the private institutions near them—or in the so called teachers' colleges which existed as public service institutions throughout the country.

The private liberal arts colleges formed a major cultural dimension of higher education. (The great private universities had in fact begun as colleges of this kind, and had only gradually and recently begun to develop the graduate and professional schools which would come to distinguish and dominate them.) Many of these colleges were founded as one important feature of the country's western expansion. Both the new communities and the strong sectarian churches of the 19th century recognized the value of having a college nearby; they saw from the start that it could be a source of revenue as well as of lawyers, doctors and teachers. These pioneers were dreaming no small dreams; every new college was to be the best in the country. Most of them took more modest directions but they survived the struggles of their early growth and by 1938 there were hundreds of them, particularly in the Midwest and the upper South. Their graduates kept them alive; it would be as hard to kill them as to move a cemetery, and they would make contributions to the country far beyond their enrollment numbers.

The teachers' colleges of the country deserve particular notice, both because of what they were and what they would become. Teachers were both essential and ill paid; it was seen to be a social duty to educate them, and this was in addition the only route to higher education for the great majority of young women. The education they offered was limited, and often devoted more to method than to the substance of the subjects that would be taught. They were condescended to, of course, by the universities and senior colleges, even though both kinds of institution offered courses in education and trained a fair percentage of teachers who went into the public schools. From the teachers' colleges a whole system of colleges would emerge after the war: the broader-based state colleges, many of which would in turn become regional state universities.

Much was latent and available for development in each type of institution. In the 50s and 60s the emergence of new institutions had been almost too rapid and casual; that limitation was less striking however than the changes in the already established places, while these in turn would be only a modest part of the educational world we confront today. With all its fumbling and decentralization, the country makes its needs clear; to judge by the variety now available to students we are determined to meet needs that are enormous and extremely complex.

The growth and change in this sixty-year period began with

great suddenness in the years from 1946 to the early 50s. No one could predict at that time how solid and even formidable the new institutions would become. Today we see an array of educational means never before available in any society. We can best understand this great change by looking at our major types of institution as they exist today; and as I do so I find that my years both inside and outside the world of formal education lead me to judgments I had not even thought of making thirty years ago.

The great universities are a unique surprise. My associations there have unusual continuity, from my freshman year at Yale to the Woodrow Wilson Chairmanship fifty years later. They did not help me to see clearly the great revolution of the wheel, however, the massive changes in nature and mission, which these places have undergone. I saw the universities shift into new government/industry partnerships under the impact of the Cold War, but I had not expected the administrative over-development, or the enormous appetite for money, which has led to endless fund-raising campaigns (each one fueled from the ashes of its predecessor). This entire bustle seems to be subsumed under some kind of corporate metaphor, where money is master and the administrative means have often grown into a structural end. Most are not as far gone as the nameless university in Boston which paid its president a percentage of his clever investment coups in addition to one of the highest compensations of any university president in the country. This distortion of the university's proper business has been paralleled in many places by a singular neglect of proper maintenance, so that we have at times the worst of both worlds, and this in places of—to use the jargon—great positive cash flow.

This, of course, is a worst-case description, enhanced I must admit by the fact that the overpaid president managed to lose a significant part of his university's endowment by forcing an imprudent investment. The point to be understood here is that money, the management of money, or the corporate style of decision-making, are not by themselves valid in defining the spirit of a university. The great university I headed in the 1960s recently launched a campaign for 1.5 billion dollars in new support. As I told the campaign leaders at that time, the amount is not the central issue; the university's sense of its true mission is vastly more important, because it alone will bring strength and growth in service. The money is only a means, and used in the wrong way it can even damage the institution it claims to serve.

The difficulties and dangers of using corporate styles of decision-making in the university setting are many, but the greatest lies in the pretense that one can quantify qualitative situations and judgments. Universities exist to further the quality of advanced thought, and any dilution of that end by false procedures and uncritical bottom line thinking dilutes and even perverts the university's mission. That phrase 'bottom line' is a prime example; it is taken to describe a result, a conclusion. It has thus become a metaphor with overtones of precision and finality. In fact the bottom line means nothing unless we know how we got there and what was achieved along the way. So with the other corporate metaphors; we must not let them fool us with their pseudo-authority. The authoritative words for a university are *creativity, integrity, knowledge,* and *insight.* These create the standard for its operation, and the basis for judging its worth.

These characteristics of the current university world are froth on the surface when compared to the intellectual and social developments which have made the name *university* a substantial misnomer. When the heavy involvement with government and industry developed, the big support automatically followed. Special research institutes, heavy grants programs, and major consulting fees all became part of the landscape, and the steady shrinking of the 'normal' teaching load can be attributed quite directly to this new climate of privilege. A special class of faculty has been reborn—the wandering scholars, like those of the 12th and 13th centuries in pursuit of the best audiences and the highest pay. The comparison is not fanciful; the current lack of institutional loyalty reveals it all too clearly. And this self-styled mobile group constantly and publicly affirms its superiority, its commodity value.

There are obvious, destructive by-products to this stance—a multi-class system for one, with the teaching burden tending to fall on the young, the untenured, the partially educated graduate students, and the so-called adjunct faculty. These young people of the graduate and faculty group are currently making themselves heard, and their resentment creates an additional force against community in the university setting. Even the elimination of a retirement age has had a negative effect on faculty cohesion. As a result, we have a range of separatist and centrifugal forces at work on the university world; they radically redefine not only its structure but also its purposes.

As I have watched these developments gain strength, I realize that much as in the 60s, the chief issues or lines of force were weaving themselves together into a new pattern of corporate institution—corporate and about to become much more so, perhaps, as the new bio-medical partnerships and technologies assert themselves in the budgetary affairs of the universities. Obviously I see great variations among the major places, but their culture, their ethos, has become reshaped and at times distorted. Once again, means have become ends, and great intellectual purposes in turn become twisted into the ed-biz, the credentials, and the network for future advancement. The universities have become in one aspect money machines. I recognize, naturally, that the money is essential for these congeries of research institutes which dominate many universities. At the same time this method of funding much of our research is a major driving force in fragmenting divisions and major departments. When a faculty member must find seventy or eighty percent of his own salary support he is not inclined to be collegial about his work. He may share the authorship but not the funding.

Under this pressure a faculty member with tenure as a largely research-oriented faculty member is at times lured into a certain amount of fraudulent research and a much larger volume of 'shared' research—in which the list of authors may be almost as long as the piece itself. These abuses of the mind point clearly to a false concept of learning in which production is measured by volume, not by content, and the 'packages' of research are so limited and circumscribed that almost by definition the large and creative questions are unasked. That criticism has been particularly obvious in the sciences, and it has also assumed some remarkable—even grotesque—forms in the humanities.

The great unresolved issue is the relationship of teaching to this seemingly inevitable pattern in today's university. The best evidence for the depth of the problem comes from the two extremes of the academic community—the young faculty, and those wandering stars at the supposed top of the hierarchy. The chronic lament of the first group: "I want to teach well, but the reward system pays only lip service to that and measures me only by my publication and visible prestige record." This is not a self-serving statement but a well-documented reality. A recent and exhaustive study of the question shows that the reality of this bias has not shifted in the last thirty years. There are pious statements aplenty, but little truth to back them up.

Evidence from the highly visible star faculty is even more devastating. The University of Illinois at Chicago has just embarked on a vigorous procurement program. The rhetoric of one of those stars procured is eloquent in what it leaves out. "In a commercial civilization honor follows pay," said faculty member Deirdre McClosky. Professor McClosky also stated, "I'll move the instant it becomes clear that U.I.C. isn't going to carry through on this [upgrading]. That's the trouble when you hire people like me...we're mobile." There is a singular lack of responsibility here, even if we set aside the bizarre definition of honor. One is not hired to serve the institution but to be served by it; if the conditions are not fulfilled, the star professor has no duty to help bring them about, and nowhere is there even a hint that students might have a right to claim some loyal service from their golden professor. It seems to be enough for her to grace the place with her presence. Or take this same question of loyalty and purpose back to the young faculty member; this is his model for professional success—one who is greedy, selfish and ultimately on a mere ego trip.

As I deal with these aspects of current university life I suddenly find my mind full of echoes. Some are from long ago and reflect the vital role of graduate school, no matter how eccentric or abused in shaping the next generation of academics. Others are from only half as far back; I hear the 60s again, with all the social and cultural preoccupations that turned those years into such a watershed for our century. We have made our somber peace with the Vietnam War, but we continue to wrestle with a second great issue, that of equity for blacks and other minorities, who still are not where we dreamed in the 60s they could be. The intellectual ferment of that period is still with us in strange and often perverse approaches to the same old human and ethical issues.

Because the major universities have so great a range of purposes they are particularly subject to the social pressures I described in the beginning of this chapter. I am not comfortable with these qualities of dispersion, but despite my regret for what is lost I have a sympathetic view based on my sense of their inevitable growth in certain directions. They have been the logical centers of specialized activity since the beginning of the Cold War, and the end of that period has obviously invited a whole new range of specialized programs and research centers to their mix of enterprises. The same must be said for the latest developments in computer communications—the realization, which even Bill Gates was a bit slow to recognize, that a full flow of information could be placed anywhere in the world. The inevitable result is symbolized by the fact that the great majority of universities now require, and often provide each student with, a computer. A substantial change in teaching approaches will result both on campus and in the universities' off-campus programs. Huge distance-learning programs are becoming a major dimension of university life, and they are a further reinforcement of the centrifugal forces that we find at so many points in the university community.

We see in today's university the mature form of those many directions that emerged in the 1950s. Research is carried on in many other places, but the demand for university sanction and staff almost forces the university to agree that one of its many dimensions should be this complex of institutes, special grants programs, government initiatives, and major individual scholarly effort. Only one aspect of full university life, it does much to shape all the rest; no other institution in our society plays a role comparable to that of the university. It is a major expression of that diaspora of ideas as well as institutions that marks the end of the century just past and the beginning of the century just begun.

If the pace of technical change is frenetic, it cannot compare in human importance with the new place of women both as students and as faculty and administrators. This change is now visible everywhere, but it is the change in perceived importance and power that is most significant. At the same time it has diffused and redirected the social order in every institution as the center of power has shifted. Even the places that have traditionally had women students now have a new sense of parity between men and women whose impact is still being absorbed. In time a new sense of community will result; at the moment major legal and ethical issues are still being debated and litigated—and salaries certainly do not yet reflect the intellectual status women deserve—and this despite the fact that money never defines true stature.

The sixty-year development in the relation of older people to the university world is not as insistent as some of these issues between men and women, but it adds a surprising element of influence. In part this is due to the presence of alumni in the financial structure of every institution, but in a far broader sense the elders remind the university of the range of educational concern that is appropriate to it. They have no axe to grind; in many ways they are the purest scholar-pupils, and the programs devised for them speak to their great breadth of concern with learning. Curiously enough, they are a potential corrective or antidote to the fracturing of community in the universities. Or, to put the matter more accurately, they are supporters of the community, not through any easy unification of its disparate strands but through the strength of the support that flows from their interest. The power of the great universities comes to a remarkable degree from the resources that the elders can bring to them. I have objected to the negative impact of any university's endless hunger for money, but its senior alumni have a consistent record of thoughtful support; in this way they give direction to the universities without being daily participants. And they do it, of course, beyond the confines of formal university structures, through the thousands of foundations large and small that nurture the national community and in many ways set its agenda. They feed our educational ventures by grants that benefit the universities, but they do it above all by pushing the envelope in attitudes and horizons as well as bricks and programs. Once these extra-mural needs and impulses directed themselves toward lyceums, then the Chautauqua movement; now they root themselves in broad and diverse formal structures of education, while they sustain their old zeal and show an often sophisticated grasp of the use as well as the great personal significance of their contributions.

These pressures from the growing community of older people are a response to the academic world and a stimulus that carries it far beyond its own formal limits. In this way they anticipate the greatest and most pervasive concerns of our culture, which have brought so much conflict to the university world today. *Conflict* is too simple a word for the real issues of value that preoccupy our society. The elders have the time, knowledge and desire to pose these issues and, through their presence and the mass of their support, they direct them toward the universities. And ironically enough these basic issues of value are more divisive for the universities than for other institutions. This is the clear result of the places that the universities themselves have become. Their dedication to field, discipline, institute has a twofold negative effect on any hope of community. First, the disciplines have their own battles of value within themselves; second, their internal issues separate these disciplines from one another and constantly work against any serious effort to think across disciplines. Intense scholarly warfare in the humanities puts immediate distance between them and the equally strenuous issues confronting the social scientists. In this way the universities concentrate within themselves the very conflicts of value that pull them apart; but that statement though profoundly critical is not an indictment. It is a simple recognition of the present state of academic thought, subject to the most intense disagreements but clearly in no position to integrate and reconcile them. Universities cannot serve this function in our society; their nature and activity now work against it. They are wonderful arenas for conflict, but not for its resolution into new order. As a result every major issue and a good many smaller ones are displayed there much as in the 60s, but with one profound difference. These conflicts have become endemic to the institution, where in the sixties the conflicts grew from society, which then used the universities for its purposes. The undergraduates of the 1960s have brought these inside, as they have become the senior faculty of the 90s and beyond. Today's issues of incivility in the classroom, sexual interaction between faculty and students, or departmental class warfare, all belong exactly where they are—at home in the university. Other educational institutions will show one aspect or another of our conflicted society, but the universities have them all, and they get them from three sources quite independent of each other but working jointly: the elders, the sixties activists now senior faculty, and today's undergraduates with their mix of immaturity and great social awareness. These three elements keep the universities in a state of constant ferment.

Other institutions are multiple, of course, not only in number but also in type—liberal arts, community and technical colleges or universities; these are a fascinating and vital counterpoint to the great many-surfaced universities. Some of this group are in themselves many-surfaced but they are urban-based, and defined by their constituency. CCNY, Temple, Louisville and dozens of others have a priceless asset; they are by definition a community of teachers and students, and they add to the communal sense of the great cities around them. With heavy teaching loads and the special counseling needs for a largely commuter student body their staff is hard-pressed, but they have one great characteristic that adds to their strength. A sizable percentage of their students are the first members of their families to go to college, and the purpose which this lends to daily life on these campuses is striking. I have had a variety of working encounters with them—one over a period of four years—and I certainly saw major failures of quality, but I also saw the strength of the commitments made.

The community colleges share many of these characteristics with the urban universities, but they concentrate on one band of the spectrum—in many cases the first two years of college. Critics say that the community colleges merely extend the years of high school and allow students in grades 10 through 12 to kick back for two more years. I see little evidence of this; the high schools themselves have major problems, but in the face of the myriad jobs they must assume it is glib and uninformed to picture the tempo there as slack or indolent. The community colleges exist in continuity with the high schools—but in doing so they help with a transition to senior college work that many students need and appreciate. Again, it is a modest and unthreatening community, but we cannot assume that its work is perfunctory or routine.

A second major quality of the community colleges explains

the tone of seriousness that I found in the visitor seminars I was asked to teach there. I saw a remarkable range of ages and purposes. These students were actively looking for a result; some had a very specific goal in mind, while some were as unfocussed as an Oxford undergraduate in the old genteel days. They were all there for the experience of it, and the uncertain ones had one quality in common with the most self-motivated: they did not feel that they were *entitled* to the best that might be offered. They were grateful for it, and few had come from backgrounds that made the opportunity of learning expected or automatic.

These institutions have come to embody the workaday patterns and opportunities of higher education; some recent studies suggest that they have more to offer *undergraduates* than some of the most highly regarded universities—with a great variety of courses, taught by faculty dedicated to this level of teaching.

Two further aspects of the community colleges are notable, because they show so clearly that education dispersed through the surrounding community at the same time draws strength from it. The average student age has risen steadily, and will soon be over twenty-four. This implies that the college is serving those who already have some kind of community life apart from it, and the faculty is drawn from that same community. This is evident because 65% of the faculty members are part-time; they must have another base of income in addition to teaching. One can of course claim that both of these conditions are drawbacks for the community colleges; I maintain instead that in this *kind* of institution part-time teachers and students can be a substantial asset. (A good deal of opposition is surfacing in university faculties to the use of adjunct and part-time faculty. They certainly see these appointments as weakening faculty status, but I could as easily claim that they are an inevitable result of the star system of senior appointments, as well as the general need to make scarce dollars go as far as possible.)

If this dedication to teaching is true of the community colleges at their best, it is a major defining quality of the liberal arts colleges—an occupation and preoccupation that still defines them. The history of the last fifty years has shown how vibrant they are in assimilating new missions and complex new responsibilities. I am particularly aware of this growth, since for some years I had a part in shaping it. My undergraduate education also showed me the dimensions of this major institutional shift—nothing less than a change of role and responsibility, with the strong liberal arts colleges carrying on enterprises that belonged to the great private universities only sixty years ago.

There is clear logic in this development. The private universities were private colleges first, formed to educate the young men who would be the lawyers, doctors, divines of their regional communities. The liberal studies of their curricula were appropriate foundations for the advanced study that would follow in many cases. (Hands-on experience—often fatal to the patient—was an important aspect of a doctor's training, while nascent lawyers learned their trade as apprentices in a senior lawyer's chambers. The colleges had a large stable of divines already in place on the faculty, so that future clerics were beginning their professional work during the years leading to the BA.)

We all know of the 19th century variations on this theme. Colleges grew up along the western and southern frontiers, almost as the necessary adjuncts to any aspiring community. (Washington Duke captured one as soon as Durham began to show real signs of life.) Like their elder Ivy League sisters, they were sectarian in character, and they were quite likely to have a 'preparatory academy' as a necessary adjunct to the college. In striking divergence from the emerging missions of the older colleges and public universities, they stuck to their original purpose and did not acquire a cluster of professional and graduate schools. One curious result of their integrity of purpose was their presumed fragility in the 1950s, as the new and expanded state colleges began to assert themselves with what seemed like overwhelming financial support. This competition had the opposite effect from that feared; with loyal alumni support and help from that new phenomenon, the private regional foundation, the colleges prospered and by the 1990s had become the preeminent places for undergraduate education. There dedicated teaching and sophisticated research are fused to one enterprise, as they should always be; and the resources now available allow a richness of opportunity and focus which the universities no longer seem to offer so clearly. I look from a distance and admire their depth of quality. The numbers of students in these colleges could never by themselves explain their influence. The *quality* of the experience and the sense of responsibility which that experience seems to engender, create an influence in the country out of all proportion to the student numbers. It may seem like academic boosterism to say so, but their sense of community has an enduring effect on the values by which their graduates live.

If there is a concentration of effort and influence in these largely residential kinds of education, I see in higher education at large a remarkable dispersion, again a diaspora of educational effort throughout the country. This shows itself in myriad ways— the years abroad, the specialized technical schools, the advanced training programs offered in many fields by industry, the wild proliferation of adult education courses, excursions, educationally defined cruises. One may smile at these, and see many of them as good money makers for the sponsors but very little more. An attentive ear discovers, however, that many of these encounters have a continuing effect on the participants that goes far beyond the brief days of the program itself.

And finally there is an increasingly rich opportunity offered by television and the computer world, the most seductive media so far invented for 'educating' their viewers in the root sense. These can lead us out of ourselves for good or ill, and by an enormous variety of explorations. They can also be codified to create courses for credit; then the medium becomes a new kind of institution, and one of particular value for those whose work or family schedules keep them from conventional adult programs.

Taken together, these special programs of education reach tens of millions of people; they constitute the greatest part of the educational revolution that I have lived with over the past sixty-year period. Education is both ubiquitous and life-long. We do not realize what great changes take place, precisely because they develop piecemeal and gradually become accepted, are constantly with us. Naturally there are problems with this great dispersal. There is an obvious overload of information brought to us by the new electronic systems, and there is great difficulty at times finding coherent meaning within the overload. At the same time, we have astonishing riches of knowledge and experience available in every field—and this not only as information but also as activity in the most diverse cultural encounters. From the arts to the most speculative sciences we are given the constant opportunity to be engaged, involved, drawn beyond ourselves to new levels of insight.

We find ourselves at a point of remarkable opportunity and risk in education and in our lives. In two major aspects the means of education are everywhere. We have technical access to incredible amounts of information, and we have work that demands constant upgrading of the knowledge we use. Both these defining pressures seem exponential; our information, like our computers, lives constantly under the threat of its own obsolescence. These create for us states of mind both stimulating and deeply frustrating. They also pose an overarching question: How are we to protect and nourish the inner meaning of experience when we are bombarded with an overload of information that turns out so often to be transient and illusory?

We must set these questions in a context of remarkable achievement in the *total* educational system. I have trained myself for some years to listen (wherever I travel) to the matters that those around me are discussing—snooping that I once thought was the most dubious kind of research. To an amazing degree these strangers are talking about some aspect of education, for both themselves and their children. Inevitably this education is piecemeal; that is a chief characteristic of our educational approach today. The coherence of it is more and more often left to the individual—which once again suggests the major task that now confronts us. This is the job of integrated thought that was once the prime responsibility of higher education. Today its institutions cannot by themselves manage that coherence; their multiple missions take them elsewhere, and we may have to look to the best of the visual and artistic media to provide us with an ethical structure to match and augment education's core beliefs. These convictions about the integrity of the inquiring mind are central both to the academic and to the activist life, but they require also that dimension of searching social and artistic inquiry at which the best of television and the living worlds of literature, art and music excel. Here the formal and activist modes of education meet; and we need them more than at any point in our past history.

The dual discipline of knowledge and informed choice is necessary for one basic reason; we now have easily available a flow of information which is virtually infinite. (At least it is infinite in the context of our power to absorb and understand.) The *valuing* aspect of education is the only stabilizing force in our society adequate to meet this flood of fact and pseudo-fact; once again, it is active, not inert; it is highly concrete, not abstract; it speaks at its best to large numbers of people, but it speaks to them individually. This defining, focusing and valuing quality of the arts and sciences is a major antidote to the excesses of our 'information age.' It is also one essential element of activist education, since it demands individual response and some type of heightened perception from each of us. As we become to an amazing extent a society of information processors we must take equal care to be a society of choosers, valuers, ethical in the sense that our personal experience is seen to be important, of consequence. One of Socrates' greatest claims was that the unexamined life was not worth living; I take him to espouse precisely the kind of activist education I am urging here.

We now meet the perennial purposes of education in a new and augmented form. The reach from Socrates to ourselves is not measured in time but in mind-set. It is not defined by an array of texts but an array of questions leading to convictions of value that then lead to action. Socrates did not have to die; those who condemned him of corrupting the youth by raising awkward questions did not expect him to die. He forced the issue, and made his ways of thought permanent in the world of thinking people. Liberal studies—his or ours—free us from the complacency of our ignorance, but equally they liberate us *for* something—for informed action and coherence of insight about the purposes which guide us.

It is essential to distinguish our searching and questioning spirit from the glib references to 'family values' that dot the political landscape today. Books of virtue and nostalgia trips in a dozen media buttress them. None of these relates to the struggle for deeper insight that I have been exploring in our culture. They are often the most dangerous aspects of an unexamined life, because they package values for easy delivery; they give us the answers without the questions. At their worst they fit perfectly the bit and byte aspect of our culture, a world of machine responses to easy questions.

I could have written another book solely about formal education today; it would have dealt with the operational problems, the conflicts, the statistics of failure and success, even the eternal question of why in this wealthiest of societies we never have enough money to do our central educational jobs *at every level.* (As we have seen, the wealthiest universities plead poverty fully as much as the public schools, which are falling apart through lack of basic maintenance.) But all of that is less important than these matters of the spirit I have addressed, both in our society and in the conduct of our personal lives. We all seek some kind of salvation, some sense of individual worth and coherence. Is that not the point where the dancer and the dance become one?

A few years ago I would have taken a negative view of this current information tsunami; I downplayed its value instead of asking, as I do now, how to use and guide it. I must remark, merely in passing, that I find the educational pundits pursuing every path at the moment—and for the most part critically—except what I now believe to be the correct one. We should take to ourselves the remarkable means of education we now have available, but we must find ways of directing those means to the best and most enduring ends of education. We must take the means for granted, and keep them from becoming ends—like communications networks with nothing important to say. As we do this we must also avoid the greatest danger of the new media, that we become passive spectators of a new kind. This was a danger of the old-fashioned lecture system, and it is an equal danger of our new-fashioned information age.

Information is not education; that is Axiom 1. Axiom 2 follows directly from it: We must, individually, actively come to grips with every major new idea we meet. The insight it has to offer is not ours until we have had a true encounter with it. Beyond this vital encounter we must then find means to organize it within a larger structure of insight. That organizing used to be the major function of the college curriculum; there is of course a great deal of contention about it today, and once again I feel that much of the argument misses the mark. The real question is not whether there is a magical collection of texts, a true canon for learning. There are *many* magical canons, and some are much more restrictive than others. My own major field, the European epic, is a whole canon in itself, but that does not keep me from espousing a pattern of education not limited by the turf arguments of the moment. Instead, I maintain that true education lies in the depth of the encounter, and the degree to which students and teachers are changed by it. That is the magic and it is a broader and deeper option in our society than in any which has gone before us. Once again, however, this dispersed, universally available education in the liberal arts will not work without our active and individual involvement. The texts and the philosophies change, but not this individual emphasis. Education is always a matter of *one*, repeated over and over but still *one*.

It is revealing to look again at the nature of the great universities. They are clearly part of the diaspora, but show it in their own way through the multiplication of institutes, research teams and major hardware to match those teams, international programs of great range and flexibility. They are educationally dispersed, and the same can be said for the liberal colleges. These emphasize their sense of *community*, however, and they have taken major steps to integrate themselves not only to their regions but in many ways to international involvements as well, by bringing these into their formal educational structure. Our society is at the same time defining, modifying and directing our institutions. The sixty-year trajectory of education has moved steadily to emphasize that our society makes more complex demands than ever before, and at every level of competence; it is the particular duty of educators however to see that we do not become a nation of highly trained but unreflective citizens. My own experience has confirmed this urgency in the decades when I have had such sustained and demanding encounter with dispersed, activist, and individual education—the three attributes that mark our society most clearly.

Moon through bare trees.
How Japanese, or might be
If we could separate the images
Of beauty and violence
That haunt our memories.

We picked them up at twenty thousand feet.
It had been a rough morning, their Migs
Death to our lumbering planes, our pilots.
We had only dive bombers left, and went out
Expecting that same hell, but
We were high, we could see their carriers,
The sky was all ours. When we found them
We found their planes on deck,
Scattered across the painted chrysanthemum,
Rearming for Midway. That flower
Was our perfect target. "You take
The one on the left, this one is mine."
I won't forget how that flower grew, and
I could see fuel lines and ammo everywhere.
The rest is history, but for me
True history started then. The flower
Turned inside out; a flaming rose
Replaced it, cultures meeting
In the most primal way. We were savages
Together, and the flowers spoke life, spoke death
Through the same voice. Only in the stillness
Of now do I begin to accept
The Zen that brought us together.

CHAPTER TWO:
The Yale Years

Part I: Young Men of Merit
1938–1942

I find myself in September 1938 on the

Old Campus at Yale where all the freshmen live. That proper name sets it apart from the new residential colleges and from the laboratories of the engineers and scientists, which are up the hill to the north. The traditions and myths of Yale rest here, in this motley array of dormitories, classrooms, chapels, offices—in every major architectural style except for the Bauhaus. I am still in shock from the great hurricane of 1938, which nearly destroyed my grandfather's farmhouse (now mine) and left me with a traumatized response to wind, which I will never lose. (This is curious, because I will still be fooling around with boats sixty years later.)

I see clearly only what is right under my nose, which means, of course, that I see only a kaleidoscope of people, schedules, unfamiliar paths and singular noises—such as the Bonesmen marching by my window at midnight. What childish arrogance, I will later realize. The real dimensions of my experience I will come to see but only over the passage of many years in a clear pattern. First there is the sheer act of growing up in the years between seventeen and twenty, which is a unique adventure no matter where one is. The arrogance, uncertainty, fitful understanding of everything will all be with me. Then there is Yale itself, an organism with a complex personality and an equally complex relation to me. There will also be a great and increasingly somber world outside, which will soon shape me and all those like me in extreme ways. Through all of it there is, for my bewildered delight and my maturing, a unique opportunity—indeed a total and living experience—of education. The boundaries of my world for the next four years are well defined.

The richness of life in a great university is never fully available to an undergraduate, either in its varied concerns while he is there or in the quality and persona it has taken on through the long years of its life. During his four years he comes to know a little of both the variety and the historic depth; he understands that his own college life has been fed by this living tradition. All of the great Ivy League universities have distinctive characters as I come to know later in my life; that of Yale is urbane, cosmopolitan in its inevitable provincialism, with the wealthiest alumni body; not as brahmin as Harvard or as "clubbable" as Princeton and dominated to an unusual degree by Yale College, which in its turn is dominated by its English and History Departments. The style of things is remarkably Anglophile, and one at least of Yale's clear purposes is the education of young men who can perform comfortably in that genteel tradition.

This phrase is unfortunate; it implies idleness, dilettantism, concern for the surfaces of culture and protection from the seamy sides of life. This implication is true but only part of the truth. The English Department is the finest in the world, for example, both in its scholarship and its deep commitment to teaching. The expectations are high but, depending on one's individual goals, these can be satisfied at various levels and in an astonishing variety of ways. (I will explore several as a student and develop others in my teaching.) The 'good' genteel tradition, of course, implies a balance among activities—again that Anglo quality—so that physical skill is highly regarded, as certainly are the 'activities' as the undergraduate culture calls them. Yale, like Princeton, has a strong southern component in its student body, which reinforces all these attitudes. Strong faculty control of the university's destiny also has a major part in setting the communal tone I will meet and assimilate.

The role of the faculty sets Yale apart to a degree from its sister universities, and it has led to growing pains of a special kind as the college has become a university. Of course I accepted· this world in ignorance, completely unaware of the arguments over the residential colleges and equally unaware of the great movement (led by Johns Hopkins) to develop a major university emphasis on research—scholarship with a Germanic influence in its structure and direction. Many Yale faculty members had been reluctant to embrace that concept fully, but it turned out that they also had serious reservations about a proposed residential college structure. (This collegiate idea sprang from the congenial British tradition, but it would call for a different grouping of the four classes, which would be…simply not Yale.)

The issue came to a head when the great philanthropist Edward Harkness approached President Angell (already suspect for his push toward full university status) in the late 1920s and proposed that he help provide the benefits of British education by funding the construction of a whole cluster of residential colleges complete with libraries, common rooms, dining halls and—of course—Masters and Fellows, some of whom would live in the College. Mr. Harkness had been extremely generous to the British universities during and after the First World War, and he felt that his alma mater would benefit from the same system. I happened to know him and had benefited from his generosity to Exeter, which had established seminar education there. I would not know for years, however, the first reaction of the Yale faculty to the magnificence of this offer. They seemed to feel that the President was reaching beyond his powers and they seemed also to be espousing that motto which has adorned faculty clubs throughout the country, "If it is not absolutely necessary to change, it is absolutely necessary not to change." They told Mr. Angell that he must decline the offer, which was too bold and innovative to suit the Yale temper.

Edward Harkness represented both a way of life and a type of philanthropy that needs to be understood better by us today. Unlike many of the wealthy men around him he did not create his fortune; instead he was educated to be a professional philanthropist, and he spent a lifetime of thoughtful, reclusive and largely anonymous effort to improve the quality of education and medical care. He did this in a highly selective way (which some call elitist today) and he weighed very carefully the larger implications of each specific gift. Most personally, he and his wife are vivid in my mind, on a bright lawn leading down to the water, (a private golf course between), and presiding over a wonderful magic show for child polio victims whom they brought from the dark corners of New York to their estate for the summer.

Mr. Harkness was a shy and in many ways conservative man, but he hardly reacted as the Yale Proconsuls and Senators thought he would. He simply went to see President Lowell at Harvard and in an amazingly short time it was announced that Harvard would have a whole community of residential Houses running along the Charles River. There is a wonderfully rich word for the reaction in New Haven; *belatedly* they began to consider what they had refused to do. In their collective wisdom they voted to instruct the President again, but this time to visit Mr. Harkness and find out whether matters might be repaired. One can imagine Mr. Angell's state of mind as he returned to that same office on the off chance that he might be able to discuss the matter. The issue was explained…at least it was described, and there was a silence. Then Mr. Harkness said simply, "Well, I suppose that I can hardly do less for my own University than I have done for Harvard." And so the Colleges were built.

This would be only an entertaining bit of academic byplay except for the fact that a whole concept of education became explicit; the buildings embodied ideas, not merely places to live. Beyond even that there was ferment in the place that it would never have again, because the whole university community would not again be caught up in a concept that affected it so visibly. The Fellows of the Colleges, for example, were drawn from every corner of the university, and they would be involved in a type of discourse with each other and with the undergraduates that had simply not been available until then.

There were other wonders; the great new library that complemented the colleges was in itself a force to shape the imagination. Its mass and central location created a heart for the university that was exemplified and embodied not only in stone but in the variety and richness of the education it supported. Again, the concept of the Colleges demanded those library resources constantly for their seminars, for interdepartmental programs, and for the individual work that taken all together established Yale's preeminence in undergraduate university education. It was truly the best of both worlds—teaching and scholarly—and only a place of large resources and equal imagination could have put it all together in such a compelling way. The novels and legends of Old Yale were by contrast the froth of things. This new Yale was substantial, flexible and yet demanding. At the time I could not see all of this, but I would come to live it in my own time and style.

Why does every writer at some point have to write about his adolescence—that transition from overage child to childish adult? Put that way, the question is the answer, of course, but not an illuminating one. Late adolescence is endlessly absorbing and indeed one prime focus for the writer's work because it provides him with unique intensity and variety of subject. That period of life is so dramatic—often so melodramatic—that he is both compelled and grateful: compelled by the action and grateful that so much of his work has already been done for him. And this reality for the writer is our best introduction to these years, in which each of us is the chief player and our little drama the chief means of growth.

College is the ideal stage for this play because so much can be acted out without too much damage. (In the world outside there is far less tolerance for growth by trial and error.) As I look back at myself, I realize that I did more of this role-playing than many around me. The gap between my mind and any coherent sense of myself was great, and I was tempted by my precocity to try on masks of maturity with no real sense of what I was doing. I was hidden from myself; worse, I did not even know how to read the signs that would tell me where to look.

A word about precocity, that most ambiguous gift of the gods: it has a curious childish side. As a boy I learned the two *Alice* books by heart. I was alert enough to language so that I realized some of the levels to which those dream fantasies could take me. I did not consciously realize that the whole transition from child to adult was being explored there, but I knew that the magic place was not easy to find, and I was beginning to sense more profound treatments of the myth beyond those childhood books. Most important, I was beginning to put myself into these discovery myths and to be articulate about them.

At the same time, I was muddled about far simpler matters than that fabled garden. I tried on a few costumes before I got to Yale, and one I carried with me as far as freshman year. I fancied that I might be a zoologist. This was the result of an unusual boyhood spent in the world of nature, with the universe alive around me to be studied and collected. I was much influenced by an almost-brother for whom that would be the right path; as a result I did not realize that my own very real interest in that natural world was artistic and philosophical rather than scientific. It would not stand up under the daily rigors of calculus or chemistry.

Nor would it survive the formaldehyde routine, a point made all too forcefully by the lab instructor in my freshman biology course. What an instructor! One day he looked us over and gave us the ground rules. "I'm here only because I have to earn my way through med school. I don't want any trouble from you; here are the lab manual and the equipment. Now go at it." Somehow the microscope and I were at odds for many years. I had had one of my own for several years; I thought I knew how to look, but whatever I saw was at odds with what our budding doctor thought I *should* see. End of dream.

Of course intellectual costuming takes many serious shapes, shapes to explore when we get to the formal educational order of my four years. Here we are concerned with that half-formed inner person who was a 'romantic scientist' but romantic in a hundred other ways as well. Do we associate conventional romanticism with adolescence because the formal romantic tradition is largely dominated by young artists, explorers and adventurers? They are like us in our late teens—they suffer the burdens of the world, but they themselves are different, set apart and therefore justified in their egotism. It is the almost obligatory fantasy that we have a unique fire in us—not appreciated by the outer world, of course, but a mark on us to be recognized by those sensitive enough to understand. Such language was certainly appropriate to me at the time; it was my major mask, my persona. Proof of it—or definition rather—was my absorption in T.E. Lawrence. This directed itself not to Lawrence's learning (though the crusader castles were romantic in the extreme) nor to the desert exploits (though they were profoundly compelling) but to a way of life that simplified everything to two rooms—one books, one music. Here was a world with nothing else to clutter life in one's search for the great mysteries. At seventeen we seldom tell fiction from reality, above all if the fiction feeds a flame inside.

If T.E. Lawrence shaped my fantasy living style, *The Magic Mountain* fed its metaphysical and spiritual substance. I could identify with Hans Castorp in his innocence, his physical limitations, and his quest to explore the most difficult questions that science, music and the body politic could evoke. To watch Hans grow gave me some inner assurance that the many encounters of my university years might have a similar meaning and result. This book turned out to be an enduring point of reference; when I was teaching the book to a group of my peers in 1997 (sixty years after my first encounter with it) I felt the relevance and compelling power again. Once it had given me a certain prospect for my life; now it was a retrospect and equally a confirmation that it gave me. Thomas Mann grew in power while T. E. Lawrence faded away.

These fantasies had many successors. As I read more deeply my images changed. By the time I was a senior my romanticism was cast in Gerard Manley Hopkins' language—*Towery city and branchy between towers.* I looked out from the window of my tower room (I had the first choice in the college room lottery my senior year) and I could see the New Haven Green spread beneath me on one side; the college courtyard was beneath me on the other with a great five panel window looking down on it. That was the year when I decided that young poets should not have desks, and I asked for and got a writing table instead. (Some years later I blushed to think of it, but it was a harmless pose at the time. When I look at it yet again some sixty years later and after two books of verse in addition to all the other writing it no longer seems like a pose at all!)

The most curious aspect of this searching time is that it is full of poses, full of behavior soon discarded, full of innocent gender encounters with fascinations quickly assumed and, if one is lucky, quickly cast off. But in among the poses is reality. In among the fashions is a style. Among the passing fancies there is suddenly love. The learning in this growth toward first maturity is intense, and it runs deeper than anything that a course or a club or a field of study could offer. It is the baseline in the whole composition of one's growing nature, and I was fortunate beyond my own awareness to live within a setting that allowed me so much freedom to shape my patterns.

The residential Colleges were a nearly perfect support system for the life I crafted for myself after my freshman year. A wonderful personal cocoon: breakfast, the white aprons and caps against the black dresses, the long morning to read and put words on paper with perhaps a class thrown in, the printed menus at lunch, a nap. Four o'clock: the Elizabethan Club for barbed conversation, a debate at dinner spilling over into the library where my closest friend and I argued about the esthetics of positivism or some other young minded pomposity. Then the two of us, apart from show time, talking the real and questioning talk that tied us together for a lifetime. (That friend is Charles Muscatine, a year ahead of me with a remarkable career in the English Department at Berkeley ahead of him. Tough-minded and courageous, he held my feet to the fire whenever my tentative insights grew fuzzy; and he still does today. What could be a better testimony to the college system at that moment in time? It gave us the space to educate each other.) Back in my room after very late coffee to write until three, the romance of the night heavy on me and the words alive on the page. That same friend said to me recently,

"You ambled through Yale, and I mean exactly what I say." It was a very special walk then; a trial and error walk more like walking down a long corridor lined with doors that opened, gave me a glimpse inside and closed again before I could enter, with the voices saying, "No, not yet; this is not the place, not the real place." Thinking back, I can almost smell this walk.

And there were girls in it; not the undergraduate affairs of the 1960s and later but innocent relationships laced with sexuality. The real meaning of these relationships was hidden from me, but what prideful pleasure to show a girl off in the college dining room, moving through the envy in every eye to some small table, her auburn hair bright under a blue cartwheel hat—all very proper, very arrogant and very young.

Some serious preoccupations and others more trivial colored my student years and also set a certain style for the future. Yale at that time took its clothes and outer trappings seriously. (This implied class distinction not visible in today's dress-down world.) The trick was to avoid the belt-in-back style or the Bond two-pants suit at one end, and the white-shoe modishness at the other. I could not avoid the subject; the women who dominated my early life were conscious of these things, and I had a real love of colors and fabrics. I read *Esquire* for trends and titillation, in time had jackets made to go with my developing taste in ties, and acquired a style that has persisted and from which I am saved only by an excessive passion for old clothes. My friends accepted this as a harmless concern and were bothered only by my zeal for shoe polishing, which they found quite affected.

To me the clothes became part of the texture and romance of the place, one small corner of "Yaleing." The university grew on me as the surfaces became familiar. Encounters and experiences of every sort were absorbed and deemed acceptable simply because they were aspects of the place. Even homosexual invitations, for instance, were legitimized, no matter how unwelcome; they came from inside the envelope, so to speak, and—at least in my case— were made harmless by that. (At the same time there was the delayed shock when I realized that I was being—not propositioned, that would be too crude—but invited; I was hopelessly heterosexual and had no interest even in experimentation.)

I was always 'looking' in that highly frustrated adolescent way which was typical of most of us. This took some hungry forms that grew out of the Yale structure. For example, certain health problems took me to the Infirmary, an old house on Prospect Street staffed by two or three very attractive nurses. They were not busy, and I was not really ill—the perfect situation for flirtations in the line of duty. One of them told me that she would like to date me, but she would have to give up her job to do it. This simple encounter was exciting enough so that I still remember her name—how revealing, that I made so much from so little.

In these many ways I was creating a special Yale for myself. I was not a spectator; in fact, I was in many ways creating a counter-culture for myself, one woven from the materials of the dominant one. This too was part of Yale's inclusiveness; I could be bohemian, write for the Lit. and arrange my daily schedule in erratic ways. If I did things well enough, if they led somewhere and were not aimless and idle, they would ultimately be accepted. In my counter-culture I acquired a considerable range of friends; obviously they shared one or more of my interests, but they did very little to educate me in the other ways of living. That became the role of a special element in the Yale culture—the Senior Society.

Societies have been for nearly two centuries a unique aspect of the Yale culture. Curiously enough the earliest were founded in revolt against the tyrannies of Phi Beta Kappa. The 19th Century was, of course, a culturally fertile field for secret organizations of every sort. They gave solidity to new communities and were a bonding force for those confronting the many challenges of the frontier (and, naturally, they were a current form of the age-old passion for clubs of every kind). At Yale they quickly became a measure of success, a final mark of distinction and a means of reaching beyond college into the wider world. Networking in short is not an invention of the 20th Century.

These are surface observations: the actual purpose and impact of relationships fostered during senior year lie far deeper. There are differences among the societies and I can speak only of my own, Berzelius (named for a great Swedish chemist). It is clear, however, that some form of structured intimacy operates in at least two of the others and equally clear from the seniors chosen that diversity of background and interest is central to the selections made. Once inside the hall—or tomb as the buildings were originally called in deference to a 19th Century sense of secrecy and romantic mumbo-jumbo—the sustaining purpose of the Society becomes clear. There are two meetings a week: a long evening with dinner on Thursday and a more social occasion on Sunday, often with an outside speaker. At the Thursday session the fifteen members (today, with co-education, there are sixteen) take turns in presenting themselves to their peers; hopes, dreams, plans and problems are available for discussion by the whole group. Inevitably a certain degree of critical analysis comes into play, and the judgment of the group must operate to control any intemperate personal clashes. In fact, one great purpose of the organization is the building of mutual respect through this process of intimate discussion. Of course it can be carried too far, but that is true of a good many undergraduate encounters. A more serious question, particularly in the politically correct climate of the moment, is that of the organizations themselves. Are they simply elitist clubs and part of a whole net of privilege and entitlement which selective higher education represents? The answer must lie in the selections made and the effectiveness of the associations formed. That is a stiff statement but it is intended to be so. If the Society cannot make selections on the basis of merit and diversity then democracy itself turns into tyranny, and quality becomes a nonsense word and worse—if it turns to this kind of leveling to express itself.

Certainly my experience seems to me sixty years later to be a complete refutation of any doctrinaire hostility. I was permanently affected by my membership and shaped in ways of civilized understanding that I surely lacked at the time. My own description of my undergraduate years is testimony to that fact. I had a remarkable education at Yale; I was beginning to define my vocation and even to practice it. I saw my elders not only as models but as companions; I needed to confront my peers as well, to enjoy the company of men to whom I would never have been attracted and to learn confidence in myself without using it to denigrate others. Everything in my life at that time tended to come as a sudden illumination. So did Berzelius. I always had a capacity for friendship, but not in the wide-ranging way that was now available to me. The Senior Society was not my most important experience at Yale, but my Yale education would certainly have been incomplete without it.

The Yale setting allowed an almost Platonic, timeless experience, but it was equally one filled with the shock and surge of The Great Depression and the coming war. As such, it was a setting of individual and social conflict beyond anything I had encountered. These high winds had passed me by until now, and suddenly I was caught up by them in all their newness, their shock effect, and their demand—above all the last. I found myself the innocent, fought over, argued with, moralized at. This resulted in part from a special counseling structure set up in the freshman dormitories, to keep order, and to do some amateur advising if it was called for. Those filling this role were graduate students and they were joined by another group of program assistants in some of the major campus organizations. In some unexpected ways these older students evoked the shape of things to come. One of them was a rabid Fascist who lived in my own entry, bedecked his room with large Nazi banners and was generally obnoxious to boot. Quite the opposite was an absolutely charming pacifist and social activist who was the assistant director of programs in the Christian organization, Dwight Hall. His name was David Dellinger and I would meet him again thirty years later as one of the notorious Chicago Seven during the troubles of the late 60s. He was unswervingly faithful to his code of dissent (as his life would demonstrate again and again) and he was a powerful force, someone to reckon with when I was seventeen. That dissenting mode in Dellinger took at the moment the form of a passionate witness to certain dark injustices and to the constant need to confront them. It was a true vocation, the first of such single-minded convictions to enter my life. Dellinger was, inevitably, in the business of arousing guilt and making converts. He was a spectacular evangelist and one could hardly deny the call; it demanded an answer. I looked at my own emerging interests—a flair for literature which I did not fully realize I had (and would spend my Sophomore and Junior years perversely denying) and an immediate sense that my tastes were pure indulgence when the world was obviously in flames. I was at a most persuadable age and my inner conflict was deeply disturbing.

This was only the first of many internal battles. The later triple tension among my teaching, my research writing and my administrative demands would be the heaviest, but this first one may have been the most important because I found a constructive way of dealing with it. I detached myself from the puzzle by imagining a contemporary with great promise as a painter. Should he set it aside in favor of the immediate and urgent causes? Years later I remembered how seriously and ponderously I argued with myself. When I finished, the answer was clear: I was able to separate a charismatic argument from a sound one. I did not at the time see how central to my education this stabilizing of my judgment was, but I would use it as a touchstone in the old alchemical sense; the base metal of a bad argument would jump out at me—at least after the first seductive moments. To sacrifice a true vocation to a dubious cause—or even a great one—would still be a betrayal of myself.

Here, then, was one live conviction to hold as I groped my way through these tangles of my growth. The demands on my allegiance took other and less personal forms, of course. A major national battle was emerging between the isolationists—honest and dishonest—and those who saw the emergent European war as an inevitable concern for the United States. This conflict of judgment led to student expressions of denial like the Veterans of Future Wars, who floated a seductive but specious peace movement—specious because it emerged after the German Russian detente but vanished in a puff of smoke—like a stage Mephistopheles—when Hitler turned east in his fateful summer campaign. It was my first encounter with political manipulation on a large scale and, like the more personal demands and surprises which Yale brought me, it aroused fears and self-doubts which I would learn to expect. At least the element of surprise would be gone when I was hit with major challenges in the future.

One overwhelming event should perhaps have been no surprise on December 7 when it hit my classmates and me. Since the generals and the President were equally taken aback, however, the undergraduates may be forgiven. For us it was of course a more significant shock than to our elders; our lives would be totally changed, forcing into focus a unique and sudden maturity which none of us could have imagined. In retrospect it was clear that on December 7, 1941 we already had a good deal of evidence about the coming war to work with, to think through. But the evidence was 'out there' and the special qualities of seventeen to twenty-one and of undergraduate life in general had kept it at bay. There was one other element; the day of Pearl Harbor was so dramatic that it created a very high level of excitement in the whole country. For me it became a much more personal moment in time.

To understand this moment fully we must go back three years. I had seen a picture on the dresser of the freshman councilor whom I admired most. He said in answer to my impudent question, "Oh, you don't want to meet her, she's foolish." (In my arrogance I did not imagine that he might be protecting her from a dubious and volatile character like myself.) The picture stayed on my mind, but I saw no way to go about a meeting. Two years later, and quite by accident (but are there accidents in these matters?) I discovered from one of my good friends that he had actually met the mystery girl through his mother, and that she had come from Smith to do graduate work in the Yale school of nursing. I promoted a dinner with them both, and liked very much what I saw. My friend dropped by the wayside, and when I discovered that Reinhold Niebuhr, the distinguished theologian, was a colleague of her father at Union Seminary I invited her to come to one of the lectures he was currently giving at Yale. I sat, thinking less and less of Niebuhr, more and more about Grace Nichols. I took her to her dormitory, came home quite besotted, and read Emily Dickinson all night—a curious love-potion, perhaps, but it certainly worked for me.

My urgent 19-year-old attentions were too oppressive, it seemed, and by late spring (as she said later) she had decided to weed her garden. I languished all summer, but at the start of my senior year a graduate school friend stopped me on the street. (Are there accidents?) "Grace Nichols was asking about you." Ten minutes later I was on the phone, and the relation that had been artificial and strained in the spring seemed quite natural and easy in the fall. Enter December 7, 1941, a true epiphany for the country and for us personally.

It was a cold, crystal day in New Haven. Grace was with me; we were at a foreign film, and when we came out we could hear the strange, totally unfamiliar sound of breaking glass (in the windows of a Japanese restaurant, it turned out). We were headed for a cup of something, and when we pushed our way through the restaurant door the mystery was solved: "The Japanese...Pearl Harbor...loss of fleet." Kate Smith was roaring "God Bless America" over the general hubbub; Grace and I squeezed into a corner. Since she was a graduate nursing student (the most demanding Master's degree in the world, I told her) she naturally thought of going into one of the hospital units that would be formed. Hours went by, and gradually "You," "I," became "We" as we started in a most tentative way to see what our lives might be if we put them together. The time was a total catalyst for us; when I left her at her dormitory we were committed. The next day I stepped out of my Greek course and started Japanese. There was a drunkenness about Pearl Harbor Day, which we would never forget, and an intensity growing from the removal of uncertainty in our lives. One might have assumed the opposite—that we would be filled with uncertainty—but this simply was not so. The maturity we were looking for in our many different ways was now upon us. We were in it—in a war, but equally in the urgent shaping of our own lives. We had been acquiring elements or foreshadowings of maturity. Now we no longer had that tentative luxury but were totally immersed in it. The recruiters came and confirmed that fact. We were to be the ensigns on destroyers, the marine lieutenants on the beaches, the mandated leaders.

Looking back I can see the innocent snobbism of that attitude. But it was also a fact of life and death. I would hear of the death of remarkable classmates and I would say to myself, "Now he is gone and he was a better man than you. How are you going to carry on what he would have done?" I would have many chances to ponder that question not only because there would be many losses but also because I would be so clearly left behind. As they told me at the recruiting table, "If we take you with your crazy heart, we will simply have to send you back." And so it was that I chose to pursue the vocation I had finally discovered.

What interaction between my fitful maturing and my formal education brought about my discovery of a vocation? I had come to Yale with a remarkable Exeter experience behind me. At Exeter I had found that quickness was by no means enough; I had developed a taste for poetry without even thinking about it, and I had enjoyed the special privilege of an extra year after graduating, a privilege I owed to being two or three years ahead of my peer group. I have already mentioned the death of the 'romantic scientist' in me. At the same time I was handed a counterweight in the form of advanced seminars in history and English. This was quite a different arrangement from the advanced placement programs now available through secondary school testing. The courses were specifically for freshmen, but they were specialized—in my case Shakespeare and European Renaissance history. Yale's great strength in the Humanities showed here. (There was faculty to spare for the project and a willingness to staff small classes with senior people.) The program itself owed its existence above all, however, to the wisdom of the Dean of Yale College, W.C. DeVane. He was in the English Department himself but his insight showed everywhere in the curriculum. He was a great believer (as he told me some years later) "in the careful application of top dressing to the young plants that were able to absorb it." He accepted a conventional curriculum for conventional students and opened the door very wide for students who could do more.

It turned out that DeVane knew about me before I got to Yale. Years later I happened to see my recommendation from Exeter, which startled me and may have caught someone's attention so that the judgment reached DeVane. Exeter was so vigorous and stimulating for me that I did not really think about my position in the school—as I would not think about it at Yale. DeVane opened the door, in any case; gradually and in a quiet way I came to know him as a friend and mentor—one of the two truly distinguished men who shaped my career. The result for me was a most remarkable freshman year. Advanced French and Greek met two requirements, that revealing and chastening year of Biology another. The two seminars held center stage for me, however. They were heady stuff and the Renaissance course had a unique dimension. It was taught by T. E. Mommsen, grandson of the great German classical historian of the same name. Ted Mommsen was not a striking teacher but he was a very good person who became a close friend during the next three years. His description of his escape from Germany and of the offers Hitler made to get him back gave substance to those great issues that were still at the outer edge of my consciousness. (They became central a few years later when Ted killed himself in a deep depression over the barbarity of the final events of the European war. He was also gay and having trouble with that aspect of his life.)

The Shakespeare course was taught by Yale's Renaissance-specialist, with the assistance of a very able and simpatico graduate student. Here the full intoxication of Shakespeare came home to me. I had read a few plays, of course, but now I read virtually the whole canon, sonnets and all. Further, I wrote a paper each week. Such exposure gave me a hunger to read massive amounts of any author's work rather than snippets from it.

Along with the Renaissance history course it opened doors that later courses would be hard pressed to match, and there was a danger in this, which I did not recognize at the time. And there was a greater danger, also unrecognized, in those deeply exciting experiences. They gave me a sense of independence, of intellectual mastery that suggested that I might accomplish much of my work in college as I saw fit rather than as others might pattern it. I now call it a danger quite accurately; my eccentric career in the next two years would prove that all too clearly. At the same time there was a rigorous intellectual game that Yale was uniquely endowed to provide me. I proceeded to explore both danger and game to an extreme degree and I was 'enabled' in this by my academic standing as one of the ten ranking freshmen. I had proved to myself and to others how easy the conventional route was; now I would try something else.

There emerged during my sophomore year a variety of ways in which I could move out on my own. The best of these oddly enough was a so-called bursary job, built into the whole college system as a way of providing scholarship students with their meals. I realized later the irony and even whimsy of calling my job a path of exploration, but so it was. I worked for the most brilliant of the young men in the English Department. Maynard Mack was at the time deeply involved with his great edition of Pope's *Essay on Man*, and I was given as my first job for him the collating of the editions published in Pope's lifetime. This meant working in the uniquely splendid rare book room where all the editions were; the task, which should have been drudgery, turned out to be a novice scholar's delight. I knew it was a privilege, and the setting created the freedom of spirit I prized.

The other major 'formal freedom' I found (and I would eventually realize what a world of paradoxes I was exploring) was an interdepartmental experiment, *History, The Arts and Letters*, which Yale allowed in those years. The concept was exciting, and I would eventually use this broad intellectual base as a vital structure for my own thought. At the moment, however, I was seduced in an irresponsible way by the dream of exploring a broad range of knowledge although I had no defined intellectual pattern for it. With very careful guidance one could have put together from the riches of the various departments a program of some coherence. I tried it with intermittent and unfocussed guidance from my friend Mommsen; I wound up knowing a little about Romanesque architecture, the early kings of France, the medieval chansons and a half dozen other ventures of this kind. Inevitably I found that the power to assimilate this in a significant way was quite beyond me. When I later used the interdepartmental pattern as a way of design for some of my teaching I was extremely careful to have strong thematic structures in place. In that way, I was eventually able to tame a dangerous tendency toward dilettantish adventures and ideas, where I moved from exposure to exposure—never pausing long enough in any one subject to confront the hard work of mastering it.

Indeed, I could have fallen into one of the worst traps a great university offers—the option of glamorous, even chic, fragments of exposure, pieces of a glittering mosaic without any pattern. I was saved from this by a series of near obsessions that were as unconventional as the shallow virtuosity of my course work in these middle years of college. I found that I wanted to read massively in the work of the writers who concerned me. No undergraduate courses offered me the chance of this but I solved the problem in a very simple way: I stayed away from class and arranged my own reading. This led once again to some ironic choices. I read all of Thomas Mann in English but, as a result, I had to make up my advanced German course during the summer (as a matter of fact and in a rather offensive example of chutzpah, I did the work in two weeks).

As I realized a few years later when I was teaching at Yale, the approach I took to my undergraduate years had some surprising results quite hidden from me while I was busy being unconventional. I had chosen to do my college chores the hard way, but I was also learning some new disciplines in the process, disciplines at a deeper level than conventional good behavior would have offered. I was choosing my own major interests—Yeats or Emily Dickinson, for example—and I was pursuing them with intensity and depth. I was testing myself to see what I could learn on my own (even though I did not recognize this while I was possessed by the intimate experience of it). And I was learning to work under great pressure whenever I chose to complete a course in a compressed form, which in fact I did with four of my five junior year courses. As a teacher I would not have recommended this to any student; in fact I would have forbidden it if I could. But it was valuable training for some of the most critical periods in my later life—periods when I would put this college 'exercise' to some very public use.

The best evidence of what I was about and where (finally) I was headed came at the end of my senior year. That whole year, despite the coming of the war, was one of intense learning, since I had finally accepted English as my Departmental field only at the start of it. At the end, of course, there would be an extended Departmental Examination. Then I would find out what my unorthodox use of my time had done for me—or against me, which was more than probable.

There had been a few indications in addition to my course grades that I was beginning to get my head in place. To my great surprise I won a prize for course work papers (I bought a coat for my fiancée with it) but the departmental examination was a different matter. It demanded a significant amount of knowledge and required it in both historical and critical modes. Pressure was to be put on my memory as well as my wit. I would always remember the days leading up to it. I didn't ask for special favors but after the adventure was behind me I learned from my dormitory neighbors that the college master had—astonishingly—asked them to keep the noise down to a dull roar for two or three days while I prepared myself.

I make so much of these two examination days because I realized on the first morning that I finally knew who I was and what I was. I found it singular that I had this experience so definitively. There should have been no time for self-knowledge, but I seemed to run on two tracks at once. My self-recognition gave me the confidence to attack major exam questions aggressively, and I recalled later that I worked and wrote in a small world of my own. I had no recollection of the room I was in, and I was not conscious of what others around me were doing. The thought patterns came together as fast as I could write, and it almost seemed to me that I had been organizing these days for years without knowing it. If one can make the outrageous statement that an examination is an Epiphany, this was certainly it. At least I thought so afterward, and those who had to tolerate my terrible penmanship in grading it seemed to agree with me.

They knew that the accomplishment was something different from a fine standard performance, and they told me so only in oblique ways to keep my head from growing impossibly large. They could not know, did not know, why it had come about that I was able to write with persuasive authority about a variety of literary periods and critical standards. My limitations were made clear to me, though, in ways that tempered the arrogance I must have shown. One of my older friends, Sam Hemingway, the benign Master of Berkeley College, took me aside with a smile and said, "That comparison of the two translations of Homer was quite something. Obviously you know a great deal about Pope's version, but your treatment of the other flowery hexameter poem was remarkable. You made a very strong case for the Victorian translator, not first-rate but full of all the romantic exaggerations of the text. I believe we gave you a 93 on that section, but we also felt you'd better go and read George Chapman." Deflation and inflation in equal quantities, and a good deal of silent gratitude that my self-confidence together with my ignorance hadn't destroyed me. Obviously I blushed over the gaffe and laughed uneasily at the result.

I only half knew that I had given myself the beginning at least of skills that would be demanded of me constantly in the years ahead: the ability to produce work of quality under extreme, often distracting and destructive pressure; and the equally valuable ability to approach complex problems in an independent and confident way. These skills and qualities of character I began to acquire at Yale. I never forgot that Yale gave me a remarkable freedom to learn disciplines that were nowhere in the curriculum. The British collegiate tradition was my great friend and teacher; now I must see my friends off to war while I discovered (if I could) how to justify being at home and pursuing my own career.

The formation of this early maturity and sense of direction was of course not seen by me at the time. There was a curious dynamic to it, a duality of character and personality, which finally reached some reconciliation. The first major element through these four years was a familiar one: the uncertainties, the poses or temporary personas, the immediate pleasures and pains, which sometimes dominated everything else. My erratic nature was the clearest outer sign of these growing pains; this aspect of my life seemed almost that of a bird caught in a house and bouncing from wall to wall as he tries the doors and windows. He is in motion that he cannot really understand or control. The second quality in this life of seemingly random motion, however, was a pattern of activities, hopes, perceptions, which actually belonged together even though they did not occur together coherently. They began as imitations of faculty I admired, writers I cared about and denials of much 'normal' undergraduate behavior. These patterns of personal style then began to assert themselves more and more strongly; they became coherent, and the imitations of a way of life became the way of life itself. I had, in fact, grown through and beyond the undergraduate world; I was somewhere else and in possession of an order of life to which I was for the first time totally suited. For the next twenty-five years I brought my discords into a harmony of thought and action. I would lose that harmony at the end of the 1960s, rediscover it with great anguish, and finally learn something at least of how to maintain it.

T h e   Υ a l e   Υ e a r s

I was in a quagmire of sensations and

feelings as Commencement 1942 arrived. Like the great majority of my classmates, I was caught up in the duty laid on us by our world—a duty in which excitement, purpose, and nameless danger were totally intertwined. I was headed as the fates told me to Boulder, Colorado to learn Japanese. Eighteen months of that and I would go to the Pacific to be a combat intelligence officer; much to the annoyance of my local draft board I was taken out of their quota and held for a cadre that would start its work sometime in the fall. Meanwhile I would scrape together what income I could by tutoring, correcting papers and the like. Naturally I could not accept the Graduate Fellowship I had been offered; I could only hope it would be there after the War.

There was another current, however, flowing through me as through so many of my contemporaries. The shock of war, which jarred us into maturity, inevitably led us to think seriously and searchingly about life after war. Many would be married in the next few months; if we survived we could already begin to imagine the pattern of obligations that would be ours. But for some of us—and I was one—there were inner imperatives of commitments to a way of life which might be ours, integral to us after the War and for the long future. We were simultaneously driven by the immediacies that lent such energy and edge to each day, and by a heightened view of our own mature direction. That was the complex and indeed ironic atmosphere generated by the summer of 1942.

Grace and I took a small apartment in New Haven but realized we could not be married until some of these tangles were resolved. Suddenly in late October the word came; I was to enroll in the late November class in Japanese at Boulder, to be a civilian until I graduated and then to be commissioned. On October 31 we were married only to receive word ten days later that every plan had been changed. I was to become a Yeoman Second Class and be flown out at the Navy's expense. I had spent our last money on a train ticket to Boulder; now I was relieved to have someone pick up the bill. Those plans were shattered in turn when the Navy rejected me at my physical exam, finding my erratic heart a poor risk for active duty. It was a bleak message but I knew that the scarlet fever of my adolescence had left me with a problem I could not control. My guilty conscience was, however, all the more aggravated because of my deep compulsion to get on with life as I had now begun to picture it. My "good fortune" was a most ambiguous gift from that goddess, as I would discover in the late 60s when the career that started in the winter of 1943 would lead me into events I could not have imagined at the age of twenty-one—events I would not have encountered if I had spent those war years in the Pacific and thus changed the tempo of my post-war life. It was some weird comfort to learn that a week after rejecting me the Navy went back to its original program, and I would have spent eighteen months studying Japanese for nothing. I would have been ordered not to use it.

Reality set in; my new wife was still enrolled in her graduate nursing program, but we must put in place some pattern of life while we waited for the Army to act. Neither of us wanted any more floating unreality and I went to work for the University News Bureau. I made a brief foray to Washington but came back thoroughly disabused of the idea that I could make a great contribution there if the Army rejected me. At the same time those inner imperatives were telling me that I should not take some immediate job if I were to maintain a longer view of my purposes.

My immediate situation never allowed me to escape the War, of course. Yale created an opportunity and a provocation, as well as a setting, for facing all of these matters—and being faced by them—and that could not have happened in one place at virtually one time except in the unique organism of a university. Its many resources were shaped to new uses, some of them so far out that they were parodies of normal university life. They had about them, in fact, that deepest quality of war, which is itself a terrible parody of the normal world, now intensified and shaped to a single purpose. The events in this period of time, and the particular experience that Yale provided, were a weird revelation of the War. They were also a superb counterpoint to that abiding nature of the university, which I was about to experience under these abnormal and often spectacular conditions.

The Army Air Force (as it still was called in 1942) quickly put a preflight school in place at Yale. A military unit has to have a band, naturally, a modest assemblage drawn from the available pool of talent. A young army captain fresh from playing one-night stands was given the job of knitting the musicians together. The result? Those of us on campus could have Glenn Miller and the finest big band in the country three times a day plus weekly parades. The spirit of our undergraduate music was translated into the idioms of war without a break in the rhythm. You had to look twice to see the historic change that was taking place right before you.

There was a black platoon in this group. Of course there was a battle over creating it at all, and there was absolutely no question of integrating the individuals of this group into the other platoons. These men were expected to fail when they got to flight school, and the Army Brass wanted them together to prove its point. Three consequences flowed from this; first, Glenn Miller created the St. Louis Blues March for the platoon and we were treated each week to a military close order dance which told every white cadet in the unit (and all of us privileged to watch) what clumsy footed "honkies" we were. Second, a fighter pilot unit was dancing before us which would have the unique distinction of losing not a single bomber under its protection during the air war over Europe. And third, a major force for integration in the country was being affirmed against the express wishes of both the military and the conservative political establishment. All of this went on before our eyes, but on those warm summer mornings we saw only glimpses of what it would mean.

The drama could just as well be personal, however, and the revelation just as devastating. One of my classmates in a shared Italian language seminar (zero to Dante in nine months) was an able and canny linguist who after the War's outbreak announced that he would go to Japanese language school. When I had been asked to do the same I had been told that we would go as active members of combat units. That was not at all what my fellow-linguist had in mind. He told the class that there were ways to stay out of the combat zone and that he was already working on them. As it turned out, the Navy Japanese school at Boulder offered him something he had definitely *not* planned on—a young Japanese woman informant with whom he became deeply involved. As the story came back to us, he felt sure that he had protected the privacy of the affair. At two o'clock one morning, however, he was quietly awakened to find that he was no longer an ensign in the Navy but a private in the Army, and within forty-five minutes he was out of Boulder and on his way to Europe. He died there trying to build a bridge across the Rhine; he would always be an extreme reminder of what could happen when the most private and most public events meet at one time, in one place and in one person.

Language and its uses led to other events cast not in a mode of Greek tragedy but rather of burlesque. When the War started, Yale had a Linguistics Department which at the level of theory and analysis was the finest in the world. The spoken language was quite another matter, of course; there was something vulgar and non-academic about that. The demands of war looked at language quite another way, of course, and the cry went up for a training program in Burmese to help us in that theater of war. What to do? We could not go to Burma, but some unsung hero realized that Burma might come to us. Up from New York came a whole crew of Lascar seamen, fresh off their ship, totally illiterate but masters in their spoken tongue—but at a cultural level which no one realized until far too late for diplomatic comfort. They were vigorous, uninhibited faculty members (they had full faculty rank); every Saturday night they got into heavy inter-ethnic battles in the local whorehouses. Every Monday morning the University Secretary—a brahmin of the brahmins—would explain to the statewide scandal sheets that these gentlemen were, "ah, a bit different from the normal run of the Yale faculty." But the language they taught to waves of fresh faced officers was all too normal; we evidently destroyed several diplomatic meetings where they interpreted in all but flawless gutter Burmese the solemn pronouncements of their elders. On the other hand, and in their own real métier at the head of a platoon, their effectiveness in the hill villages was remarkable. The villagers had been brutally treated by the Japanese, and when they heard their own idiom so fluently spoken they came out of hiding to help advance us on our way north. Of course the job was over one fine day, and our Burmese faculty found a ship again in New York. They were never the same after that, and in a far more important sense, neither was Yale. The study and use of living languages had finally proven its worth.

Of course the War brought many self-revelations within the university setting. One of the most bizarre came in the person of a professor of classics who had faithfully persisted in his National Guard duties all through the 1930s. Suddenly, at the War's start he emerged on campus as Colonel Welles, complete with boots and swagger stick. What film these came from we never knew, but there was no doubt about the fantasies he had built up during all those years of patient drilling and routine advancement. He expected an assignment as the overlord of all the special programs that war was bringing to the university. As a result, he began to prepare his persona to take in these varied units and to tell those in charge how matters should be handled. One day he made the spectacular mistake of chastising the benign Master of Berkeley College where a group of case-hardened NCOs were living during their special training. "Don't you know that in time of war a failure to impose proper discipline is an act of treason?" (They had been going over the wall after hours for a little beer and conversation.) Sam Hemingway, the Master, told me that he said to the colonel, "Brad, you can go right straight to Hell." And then he did one thing more. He called his friend the President of Yale and suggested it was time for the nonsense to stop. Charles Seymour used a chain of command that our colonel had forgotten; he called his old friend and classmate Henry Stimson, the Secretary of War. Our Colonel found that at last he had firm orders; he was to go to Mississippi to whip a new black regiment into shape. In a short time the regiment whipped him.

These four vignettes are images of a time in which life was larger than life, events had immediate consequences, and everyday happenings suddenly had unforeseen urgencies. They reveal the abrupt, even savage, transition from a peacetime society to a wartime one. The styles and customs that we knew, those that had given substance to our undergraduate years, were blown away. After four years of life-consuming war something quite different would take their place—in the same buildings, even sharing some of the outer forms of the past, but in the national scheme of things shaped for new purposes and new mandates.

My graduate years were defined in a curious way by the contrast between the tempos of war as these vignettes evoke them even in a university setting, and my deep personal involvement in a wholly different life and purpose. I was a grateful beneficiary of the constant tension between war and the graduate experience. Above all, I was forced by the contrast to recognize the unique, central and defining nature of graduate education. It is the advanced division of the university that does not serve a profession. The world of learning is its profession. The greatest war cannot change this obligation, nor separate the integral relationship between teaching and research.

That sense of the fusion between research and teaching would one day guide my administrative work as well as my own teaching commitments. For now the time was one of Arcadian pleasure; the constant presence of the War could not destroy the sense of ease and excitement fused that anyone feels when she or he first finds a close fit between person and persona. Though the War was a counterpoint to my daily life it was not and could not be the center. That center was a remarkable experience, which lived in contrast both with the War and with the nature of my own undergraduate education. I had finally come to some understanding of those past years. Now I was to explore and develop a firm and disciplined life, which had to be in many ways an opposite of my past.

I did not see this contrast clearly at the time because I was looking so single-mindedly at the new world I had entered. My undergraduate years had opened doors to a steadily expanding but eclectic and scattered view of reality. Now I would be taking eight 'courses' which might better be called areas of concentration—eight rather than the twenty or more of my undergraduate years; at the end of two or more years devoted to that concentrated effort I would be turned loose to do a piece of independent scholarly work. During this period (which was as tightly scheduled in my case as it could possibly be) I would go through the phases of Apprentice, Journeyman, and finally, if I was very fortunate, Young Master Craftsman. Analogy to a medieval guild is not trivial; there was an ecclesiastical element as well—or rather a monastic one.

The intoxications of this new world were many; I intuited them and fantasized about them as apprentices do. While a college senior I had already dreamed my connection with the learned world through Hopkins's great Oxford poem. Now I felt free to associate myself with the whole learned tradition of Western Europe. This went so far indeed that a dream image began to take shape and become a regular visitor. I would smile at this, but many years later I would still find myself in a dark northern world—dark but with enough light so that I could see the silhouette of the town across the river from the spot where I stood. It was the Renaissance north—clearly not Italy. Weirdly enough it said to me, "This is a place of learning, this is what it feels like, you belong here." Even the river functioned. I must cross it in order to get to the place I yearned for. The real and daily graduate world said the same thing to me through the depth of the work required and the enormous range of learning implied beyond it. I had been a student all through my boyhood, but now I found myself in a setting where the act of knowing was an event in itself—a way of using the mind that could lead one to understand certain issues, texts, ideas, better than anyone else had understood them. Put that way, my excitement sounds aggressive and acquisitive, but I did not feel it so. It was competitive in only one way and that was a way that others could not see. I was competing with myself. How much could I learn, how would I organize that learning, what direction should it take to make it significant rather than merely one more example of Alexander Pope's 'Learned Lumber in his head?' I would have trouble with this aggressive attitude in my later life when others at times viewed the excitement I felt as a mask that cloaked ambition. But here, at the start of graduate school, it turned into an inner enduring principle for me. There would be several guiding discoveries, but this would be primary. It was not only a central awareness for me but also an ideal for graduate work at its best.

The full scope and meaning of the graduate school in a great university is of course largely hidden while one is immersed in it. I would describe the experience as one of self-discovery and great joy in the daily work. That was certainly true for me, but because it was so I failed to understand how burdensome it could be if one had to teach the most routine courses in order to put bread on the table while one did his graduate work. Secure in my Fellowship I could idealize the experience, while many of my peers were forced both to extend and debase it. In neither case were the reality and centrality of their experience clear to them. Those years often felt like drudgery; often they were.

The graduate school experience was diluted and cheapened for them. It is, in fact, the one place where teaching and research can meet in their full intensity. The current university elaboration of institutes and specialized programs tends to diminish its scope but not its unique nature. The professional schools have clear purposes; undergraduate education in the university setting often prepares students for that professional experience. Only the graduate school prepares its students for a full life of teaching and research as one integral experience—an experience which at its height is the life of learning. Chaucer's *Clerk of Oxenford* has become such a cliché that we fail to appreciate the power of Chaucer's statement about him, "And gladly would he learn and gladly teach." First it is *glad*, a choice freely made, not for profit in the world's eyes but for its own sake. Learning for a profession is in another world from learning *as* a profession. Second, learning and teaching are inseparable; learning dies if it is kept to itself; and worse, it withers because it denies the community of scholars. And that community is clearly what Chaucer implies; he is simply reminding us of what every true teacher knows. We become learned—and possibly even wise—only through our interaction with our students. Of course this also takes place with our peers, but they are competitors while our students can be as open and disinterested with us as we are with them.

This community is central to the idea of a university, for a reason that is superficially a paradox but at heart both basic and undeniable. Every other advanced school or division in the university is instrumental in some form. The ideal graduate school may give instrumental training but at its heart it celebrates the acts of learning, knowing, exploring—not for some particular use but for themselves alone.

We often call a particularly fine mathematical solution to a problem *elegant*—that is, it does not use one step more in its solution to the problem than is essential. In this way it is like a good poem or a fine painting—it is complete in itself; it carries its own meaning within. That same quality of self-sufficiency is present in good scholarship; we celebrate it for what it is, what it illuminates, and not for what it does. That one quality makes it central to the definition of a coherent and cohesive university. Let me be quick to say that we do not often achieve this level of quality, but if we do not hold it dear the university falls apart into a mere cluster of schools and programs designed to serve some external purpose.

What then goes wrong? I have indicated the burdens placed on individual graduate students by the need to survive economically during graduate study. This problem is intensified, however, by the attitude of graduate students themselves, and particularly so in the humanities. The average length of time for completing graduate work is between six and seven years; even before the recent tight market for junior positions there was little encouragement to move along, to work within a stated time period. The project and the degree itself are devalued by this slackness; the graduate schools in this one major way suffer by comparison with their professional school counterparts, which keep the student tightly focused. Even this is not the heart of the problem, however; the degree has, over the past fifty years, become too largely a union card and even an exalted meal ticket; as the universities themselves become more corporate and less collegial this doctoral degree—the most fragile and the most subject to debasement—

has suffered severely. The recent assertive demonstrations by graduate students have put the matter in sharp focus. They point out that they are employees and should be recognized as such. University administrators have been mealy-mouthed in their responses. They pay lip service to that high concept of graduate school I espouse, but they are for the most part not committed to it any more than they are committed to the idea of unified teaching and learning. Numerous studies over the last thirty years— such as that in the spring of 1998—have pointed out the hypocrisy of the university attitude toward teaching. Just as it exploits its graduate students, so it corrupts the full meaning of its highest degree. As a result, the word *scholar* itself loses its meaning and sense of high calling. (The very persistence of this problem makes clear its severity.) And the resistance of the senior faculty to the recognition of it becomes crystal clear if you look at the real standards for promotion; almost universally junior faculty report that their teaching carries virtually no weight in promotion and tenure. There are many reasons for this attitude, now crystallized into a policy, but the most important is a conviction that the public reputation of the university rests only on its broad scholarly reputation. This overemphasis on one aspect of the full nature of learning betrays the whole graduate enterprise.

There was in the pattern as I experienced it a steady heightening of excitement—first in requirements such as Old English, which would serve as an immediate barrier to those wanting a comfortable kind of graduate work without tears and leading to a terminal MA degree. A world-renowned graduate department like Yale's looked with polite scorn at these students, who were allowed to drift along as they wished. (Four courses and $20.00 would buy you the degree.) For the serious ones there was a second linguistic requirement and heightened expectation of performance, which usually demanded a certain amount of extended research/criticism. Beyond that there was (for me at least) the enormous luxury and excitement of a course designed to sharpen skills for the dissertation itself.

Throughout this sequence there was the illusion of a natural progression, which was, in fact, a carefully planned steady heightening of demand—a testing of the self that never permitted a sense of satisfaction. There was always more to be done than could be done, and the standard instruction was, "See what you can do with this in the next two weeks."

This approach had many purposes, but chief among them was the purging of vanity and self-congratulation that so often accompanies the little triumphs of undergraduate study. This lack of boundary was the most remarkable contrast between the two levels of learning. There were finite goals in the undergraduate years, but now I faced an attack by the infinity of knowledge. That was the pressure which forced me back on myself, so that the battle became an inner one and the guidance of my elders turned into 'tough love' of an extreme form.

One story will confirm this progression and the rigors that it brought to bear on the individual student. A few years later, as a junior faculty member, I attended a crucial meeting of the graduate faculty in my Department. I had been a reader of a dissertation which produced a highly unusual—virtually singular—response of rejection by all three readers. There was much consternation at this, and the most softhearted of the senior faculty urged that the failing candidate was merely immature. It was quickly established that the fact of his age could not by itself create an excuse. Then one of the most judicious of the full professors stood up. "We must recognize that we are at fault; we have failed this young man. Several of us had the chance in our courses to put him to the test, to assure ourselves that he should be allowed to run this risk of writing a dissertation. We are the guilty ones, and now we must give him a realistic, honest view of himself."

I never forgot that in this one event I had seen and heard the heart of serious graduate study; I also saw that it was the heart of all university education. This was academic intellectual life at its best, because it was most rigorous and most self-searching. This was the ideal, or at least a non-personalized view of what graduate education might be. And it is this high expectation that allows us to take graduate education as the university's intellectual center.

But what was it like for me to inhabit the structure and content of such a patterned world? The discoveries about myself which I had made by the end of my undergraduate years seemed to flow without seam or ripple into the action of graduate school. It was immediately clear to me that I was—quite apart from the brooding presence of the war with all of its induced guilt— superbly placed to do what was expected of me. As a result, if I had been forced to state one overriding quality of these years, it would be joy. I was embarrassed at this only because it seemed such an unlikely way to react to the demands of the finest English graduate program. It was not an easy experience in the trivial sense; but in that deeper ease which combines self-assurance with effective daily effort it was an easy time.

It even had its drolleries, one of which surfaced after the required Old English course (which turned out to be a remark- able and detailed encounter with *The Beowulf*). I was then expect- ed to take at least one more advanced linguistics course. I had never included linguistic change patterns at the heart of my inter- est in literature and metaphysics; as a result I was overjoyed (not too strong a word for my feelings) to find an escape hatch in the form of a catalog footnote: "A graduate level course in Latin or Greek may be substituted for the customary advanced course in Old Norse or Old High German." I was qualified in Greek and went hunting. Again in the fine print I found what I was looking for: "a year of study in the major Platonic and Aristotelian texts." When I pushed open the door of a large office on the seventh floor of the University Library I found working inside the most distinguished Philo scholar in the world. After laughing at the effort it had taken to find him *and* the course (he hadn't taught it for twenty-five years and originally invented it to fill in his sched- ule) he said that he'd enjoy reading with me. And so we did; the course included inevitably a good deal of English and many eccentric trances by my mentor, who was remarkably learned in a dozen fields. I got a great deal from it and was not too curious about the possibly negative attitude of the senior faculty. Evidently they didn't think that such freedom was wise; they wiped out the classical option after that year.

Even the urbane and distinguished Chairman of the French Department could show this same rigidity in a way that amused me at first but left a lasting bad taste. As part of what would now be called graduate work in Comparative Literature I took that

Chairman's course in the great classical century. There were only three or four students and one afternoon I felt enough at ease to raise the question in French: Horror; objection. "But you're not French, not in the Department—you should not be trying to speak French." It would take years before I would understand the linguistic chauvinism behind this, but I knew that it ruined the atmosphere of the class for me. (Furthermore, simply as an encounter with the Mandarin attitude to learning it was quite spectacular.)

These events were minor and almost whimsical in the context of the real flow of my work. The wonderfully gifted teacher–scholar Maynard Mack, for whom I worked as an undergraduate, was teaching the course in the Augustan Age. It provided a degree of rigor, discipline and guidance unlike anything I would experience again. I was given an absolutely major assignment—to do a critical and historical analysis of Pope's *Essay on Criticism*. The subject was open ended, obviously, and on the face of it impossible to encompass. I gave it everything I had to offer at the age of twenty-three; it came back to me, with a covering page filled with detailed criticism written in a hand so minute that one had to decipher it. As I did so, my heart sank lower and lower, for every obscurity, every omission was laid out before me—I had nowhere to hide my head. Then at the bottom of the page, one line: "So far as it goes, this is the finest thing that has yet been written on the subject." The phrase "tough love" had not been coined, but I knew what it meant. I always kept that paper to remind myself of the evil of easy standards and partial accomplishments: I never found a way to express the enormous gratitude I felt for such meticulous criticism, both at this point in my graduate career and even more so—if that were possible—in the extended help I was given with my dissertation.

Virtually every graduate student who finds that period of his life rewarding does so in good part because of an unusual mentor. In most cases that mentor cannot be as remarkable as mine was. (Fifty years later he received the first MLA award for his lifetime of scholarly and critical achievement.) But no matter the quality level, the *concept* is essential; the great medieval apprentice pattern is still alive in the years of graduate study as nowhere else in our society. It creates a community, it gives (or should give) a guarantee of quality and it confirms the essential continuity of the learned world. Described in this way it has elements of an ideal environment, but the principle is essential to the success of the graduate venture.

This care of young scholars could take remarkable forms; a special course was designed to prepare advanced students for the independent work of the dissertation. The eighteenth century scholar who taught it was also a highly eccentric bachelor with buried but lively sexual interests. He had recently been consulted, weirdly enough, by one of his best junior faculty members, who found himself overwhelmed by the charms of the most aggressive young seductress in the department. She was clearly in the business of collecting scalps and the aging bachelor had known that game well for years. He sized up the situation and announced that his advanced seminar students would be taught individually in this particular year. There were two rumors: one that he was protecting me from this powerful Circe; the second of course that he wanted to keep her for himself. Either way, the decision added flavor to life during that year.

And the course itself probably gained a good deal to make up for my obvious loss. The senior professor was both a superb teacher and a deeply generous man. He was not always rigorous in his own work, but he had a remarkable flair for teaching scholarship—an unusually difficult thing to impart. After several minor forays he came into the seminar one day with a bound volume—clearly 18th Century—which he proceeded to tear apart as I looked on in horror. Tossing one segment at me—a coherent one it turned out—he simply said, "Go away, come back in two weeks and between now and then learn everything you can from what I have given you." It is a matter of note that he did not say, learn everything you can about the piece; he went much further. Those two weeks turned into my first published piece of detective work. This particular kind of scholarship was not to be my major interest, but I never forgot the excitement of that chase. It did a great deal for my tenacity and something for my ego as well. It took me out of the apprentice class for good—exactly what my old friend planned to do for me.

In sharp contrast to this level of testing and demand the oral examination was a solemn game. In the Yale of my time it was not meant to be definitive, though there were poor souls who over prepared and in a few cases actually fainted away at the first question. The most formidable aspect of it was the shock of meeting eight full professors at once; I happened to take the exam in such a way that I got the whole crew. Maynard Mack, who would direct my dissertation, was to be away for a year; it seemed wise to get the orals behind me in the spring of my second year so that some joint planning could be done. Looking back I am appalled at my cheek to ask for the examination on three days' notice, but at the time it seemed the sensible thing to do. I was given an hour of questioning before these gods went about their great affairs in private session. Much of that time was a blur, but the last question I would never forget. I had not taken the graduate Shakespeare course, in good part because the interests of the senior Shakespearean, C.F. Tucker Brooke, were so antagonistic to my own. Now he offered me a beautiful and unavoidable trap, a very neat piece of academic revenge. "Would you mind telling us what Shakespeare's *Tempest* means?" The questioner had the style of the White Rabbit but a quick and malicious mind. I was a toy in his hands, a bug on a pin. After a while they let me go and (as I later learned from a friend) my eccentric bachelor teacher Chauncey Tinker leaned over and said, "Tucker, could you have answered that question?" "Of course not," snapped the White Rabbit, "Of course not." I stood in the hall thinking all the bright things I had had no chance to say. Then the Chairman came out with a clear twinkle in his eye. "I am instructed to tell you that you have passed your oral examination. None of us has the slightest idea what you know." And with this dismissal a relieved but deflated journeyman made his way home.

The dissertation was quite another matter. Chutzpah had no place in it; I could not run on nerve and quickness to bring it off. I had, indeed, to be immersed in it in order to find out why the dissertation is the necessary capstone of graduate work. Capstone is the wrong image, however; the dissertation is inherent in the whole graduate enterprise. In the truest sense it is a rite of passage; you and your life will not be the same after you have completed it. I had a superb subject, which my mentor handed to me; Pope's translation of the *Iliad* raised many major questions, permitted many approaches and types of analysis, was controversial and subject to severe criticism of several sorts; in short, it would be a privilege to work on it. As was so often true in my later life I set out without realizing the clear pathway while I was walking it. My teaching career would show me how great that gift of a subject was. For now, the execution of the job at hand was all that mattered. A dissertation may become many things, but first and last it is a discipline—in my case a discipline with a very tight time structure as well as multiple linguistic, poetic and critical demands that took me beyond my current level of ability at every point. I had hurried my orals in order to be free for this concentrated effort. Now I must complete it in eight months since I was determined to start teaching in the spring of 1946. I already knew the generalities of the subject, and I was fairly well informed about the scholar-critics who were prominent at Pope's time (and would, indeed, contribute a great deal to the notes which Pope himself wrote). I must now establish a critical position of my own from which to interpret the remarkable English poem that Pope had created from Homer's Greek.

The very insistence of the schedule worked in my favor. My total immersion in the poem allowed each aspect of it to feed the others, leading me to an understanding of Pope's considerable learning, preoccupations, concerns and finally his interpretations of the original Homeric order—this last pointing in turn to my own growing sense of the extremely high level of English poetic order that he had achieved. All of this would lead a few years later to my first book, *Pope and the Heroic Tradition*. But at the moment, my overriding concern was with the process of making all aspects of the subject flow together. My later judgment about the importance of this effort never wavered. I cannot imagine a better way of achieving depth of independence and confidence in one's power to meet major expectations. The toboggan ride of graduate school reached its full speed and exhilaration here at the end. I never sensed the negative possibilities of graduate school since in the flow of my graduate experience nothing was negative for me. I started teaching in the Spring of 1946 after the most idyllic three years of my life. The dark irony of the situation was not lost on me, however, since many of my students for the next four years would be returning veterans.

I referred to these years as Arcadian; there was in them a whole way of life which justified the word for Grace and myself. Like so many others who marry young we did not really know each other well. After we had weathered the shifts and changes of the first few months our world began to evolve a pattern. I had my Fellowship for the second term, and in June 1943 Grace graduated from nursing school. She immediately went to work for the New Haven Visiting Nurses' Association. This was a remarkably varied job, and we discovered that it ran very well in tandem with my work. The Macks found a third floor apartment for us across the street from them—perfect, as they said, for us to be their babysitters. We had lived in three miserable temporary places—though this had not ruffled our relationship—but it was good to settle down.

We discovered that we were frugal (even when we did not have to be), very task oriented, and happy with a life of firm routine and very simple pleasures. We had more disposable income than we would have during my first few years of teaching, and we saved nearly half of it. (In 1946 we were able to buy cheaply a large, ancient black sedan that had for years belonged to a local funeral establishment.)

Our daily pattern was quite unvarying, and many might find it too rigid, too unadorned. In this way it was in the old idiom of pastoral, however. One of our first investments was in two bicycles—secondhand but sturdy. At 8:15 every morning we hit the road for the 15-minute ride to Grace's office and—three minutes later—my wonderful carrel in the Sterling Library. This was open at first, but after a few months a locked one turned up so that I could leave my work spread out. We met at home at 5 o'clock, unless we went shopping—which we did in all kinds of weather even though the bikes were treacherous in the rain, ridiculous in the snow.

Wartime diets were naturally limited, but we carried that simplicity a step further. There was a good deal of carrot salad in our program, Spam and cheap hamburger, much bread, many potatoes. Grace did it on a budget of $8.00 a week, which was also the cost of our rent. (Since both my Fellowship and Grace's salary were worth about $1,500 a year, we were well off indeed.)

We also made many discoveries in the secondhand markets. A wonderful furniture maker sold us two old bureaus from a group he had collected for the wood, and one day I made a remarkable find—the Original Yale Misfit Clothing Company whose name was glorified by a note in the *New Yorker*. The owner, Morris Widder, became a true friend as well as my outfitter. He bought clothes from the wealthier Yale students, who sold them for ridiculous prices in the spring since they expected to be outfitted again come fall. Morris kept me respectable; I recall a fine herringbone suit—seventy-five dollars at Langrock's—which he sold me for ten, and there were several jackets which more or less fitted. He used to call me Rags, and we were friends for more than ten years. Alas, his frequent depressions finally overcame him, and I arrived in town one day to find that he was gone—a fine violinist, a generous man, a wonderful part of my graduate years and beyond.

These were the elements of our Arcadia—significant work for us both, simple lives which we relished, and the wonderful discoveries along the way as we saw more and more clearly how suited we were in our tastes and convictions. It was very good, and it flowed naturally into the start of my teaching years. Given the pace and complexity of those post-war years to come, our Arcadia was about to vanish; in the euphoria of 1946 and springtime we could not see how great the changes would be. For us the three years had been a wonderful apprenticeship, not only in our two professions but also in the simple joys of daily life.

T h e Y a l e Y e a r s

Part III: And Gladly Teach
1946–1953

Why be coy? Nothing would remotely

compare, I thought, with the heady conclusion of graduate school. There was the dissertation, discreet in blue buckram but bursting in the pride of all its author's best thought and highest hope. There was the doctor's gown, with its three velvet stripes; there was the commencement program with each individual subject of doctoral work spelled out for all to see. Innocent pleasures, not the earth shaking events we thought they were at that moment but a measure of our power to discipline our effort and bring it to some conclusion. If we are truly fortunate the work may even be a bit of what it is supposed to be—'an original contribution to knowledge in the field.' This is the moment for ego, though it may take years for the deep uncertainties, the stress of sustained effort, and the whole emotional content of the degree to settle into place. I remember the recurring nightmare; in some obscure and awful way I was stuck with Kafkaesque requirements still to be met. I would wake up in a cold sweat. "It's mine, they can't take it away from me." It was, as a total event, one of the great rites of passage.

And there is a twin to this day of triumph, with a masked face and an ambivalent gesture. The teacher's obligation is known in its worst form if the years of graduate school are burdened by the drudgery of the teaching assistant, teaching, seeking to earn the necessary pittance of support. It is quite another and far more intense matter, however, to confront that first day of teaching with high hope and equal fear that one may not be able to do it well; there may be a dreadful failure in store for the teacher and the taught alike. 'I will have nothing to say, nothing to ask; they will laugh at me and go away. I shall sit there alone at the much abused desk and know that after all this work I am in the wrong place, the wrong career with no exit.'

It is morning, an early class; I go down the stone steps because my classroom (I had never been in this corner of the campus before) seems to be in some kind of semi-dungeon. I open the door, look across the room at the half windows. They are barred. Good Lord, do they give these to the new teachers so the class can't get out? I hear footsteps—many footsteps; they come all in their navy seamen's uniforms and looking seven feet high. It is spring of 1946 and the Navy is mustering out some of its unneeded men by giving them a term of college. The real G.I. Bill influx will start in the fall but these men are being parked at Yale for a semester. They have not taken the usual admission tests—they are simply there. I give an assignment in the book of prose and poetry they are to use. These many years later I cannot remember at all what the assignment is but I can remember the rising tension inside and the feeling that I must give them a ten-minute quiz so that I can establish some control over this remarkable group of youngsters. I now realize that they are really raw recruits whom the Navy does not want to train since they are the last in the pipeline. When they come in on the second day I say, with an arch attempt at humor, "Well, gentlemen, the party's over..." but before I can mention a quiz a voice in the front row asks the first question, I grab at it hungrily; then there is another which provokes still a third. Suddenly the 50 minutes are up—I give them some clues about the next assignment and watch as they go chattering out the door. I draw a breath; I hadn't gotten through all the points I had so laboriously planned, but I did get into a lot of the good stuff. They were taking it and asking for more. And so was I, so was I. One class and I was hooked. More than fifty years later and after a career that had led in several other improbable directions, I was still teaching and as much in love with it as ever.

The exuberant tone of the whole student body was a great encouragement to my teaching. It was driven by those who returned as veterans and pulled the 'normal' underclassmen along with them. As a group they had money: again something quite different from the small wealthy segment of a standard class. They were free to consort with the local prostitutes, and if that was their style, they did not conceal it. (In fact, two of them set a young lady up in business, which was too enterprising for the authorities.) Games were much in vogue—the turning of old hearses into party cars, or the formation of temporary clubs like The Yale, Ale, Quail, Chowder and Marching Society, which lived up to its name both publicly and lustily. None of this ran counter to the high intensity—the urgency—of the work being done. It was a complement instead, created by a community of men who had learned to take their pleasures and their work in the most heightened ways possible.

And there was that other group of special people, those who returned as married students, often with children and thus an outer urgency to match that of their single fellows. There were enough of them to form an active subculture; surplus Quonset huts were turned into a village of little houses—and little they were, one half to a family. There were contests for the most imaginative uses of those little caves (as they seemed) and certainly I never heard a complaint from anyone. They did, however, have some educational impact on those second-class citizens, the eighteen-year-olds who were admitted in the fall of 1946 in parallel with the older group and of the same numerical size. The mix was very rich indeed. Not until the admission of women would Yale see anything as exciting.

This was in every way the beginning of a remarkable period in American higher education. My excitement at finding my true vocation was only one tiny personal part of an explosion in activity caused by the coming together of many major forces and events. Among these were: the pent-up demand for education which naturally resulted from the five years of war-caused delay; the enormous opportunity of the G.I. Bill which would lure into college 50% of high school graduates (and women as well as men); the greatly increased aspirations of minority citizens brought about by military experience; the prosperity after the War's end which made higher education not only feasible but sensible, as it fitted graduates for careers in that utopia which was to be the post-War world. The imagined society that was to justify and exploit all this feverish activity in education looks quaint and at times deliberately perverse from our vantage point. Its most speculative and provocative form was elaborated in a *Fortune Magazine* study published in 1955. There eleven leading public figures indulged themselves in the great indoor sport of "Futurism"—the projection of future reality based on an extension of current political, economic, artistic, and technological trend lines. As the editors said, the concern of the book and its authors was not only to scrutinize these extensions of the present but also to take firm positions about what should be true as well as about what was likely to be true.

The great weakness in such a two-tiered effort was revealed by its title, *The Fabulous Future*. There were major problems but little about finding solutions to them; indeed they seemed to add to the upbeat character of a time when all good things were possible. In higher education heightened activity was essential, given the new attitudes and expectations toward post high school study. We must prepare ourselves for a world in which the use of leisure would be our major problem; education would show the way in this as in all of society's other concerns.

There was certainly no doubt about that national venture in the years of the veterans, from 1945 to the early fifties. The impetus given by the G.I. Bill was far greater, far more multiple than anyone had calculated. It raised educational expectations in many groups, which could not have had them without this open invitation. It was the country's way of expressing its gratitude, and the universities and colleges carried out that purpose in a style that could almost be called festive. The crowding and the dislocations were accepted as the necessary conditions of a time so full of hope. These great expectations were not blighted by the Iron Curtain and the start of the Cold War. There would be dark times beyond all prediction, but it would take 20 years before they showed their true nature. In the short term these years were a time of fulfillment and great educational anticipation. Its character was marked in three chief ways, and all three would exert a major shaping force on higher education well beyond the immediate period.

The first resided in the nature of this "new" student body. The veterans set the tone of college campuses; they were obviously mature—some disturbingly so—and they asked constantly about the purpose and value of their educational experience. They took nothing for granted; they were wonderful to teach, as a result, but never comfortable or docile. They brought urgency and purpose of the most positive sort; the undergraduate world would have been transformed if college communities could have sustained this energy after the veterans left.

What they did leave as a transforming attitude was a far higher expectation than ever before: that college and university education might be available for the asking. That was a second major quality of the immediate post-war years; education shifted subtly in the minds of a million students and became a right where it had formerly been a privilege. The third was a special variant of this quality; for students it meant the dawn of a great hope that past injustices might be remedied. For the mass of white students it showed rather as a naive and uncritical assumption that if education was good then more education was automatically better. For black veterans and their juniors, college was the open sesame, the magic that would make the endless promise of these immediate post-war years available to all. It was a time of remarkable expectations in technology as in politics, and education drew its optimistic surge from both.

One obvious effect of these urgencies was a major increase in the type and number of institutions, with the development of community colleges, state colleges, state universities—all in addition to the long-established groups of public and private institutions. (And of course many of the teacher-training colleges were now enhanced in name if not in quality.) There were vast increases in funding for all of this—a utopian expectation that with money, higher education could be made both available and effective for everyone. This was an uncritical judgment of major proportions; adequate support for such proliferation was never thought through and developed. (Forty years later the consequences would still be with us.)

As a society we had enormous and uncritical confidence in ourselves. Victors in a war of staggering dimensions, rebuilders of Europe and Japan, our emotional tone was such that it would have seemed trivial and anti-American to ask restrictive questions about education or any other social activity. We felt the greatness of our resources; how could more education be a bad thing? Like adequate health care, it was almost an axiomatic next step in the development of our society. We seemed to have few fears about embarking on both of these major developments, and we certainly did not feel that they called for disciplined long-range planning.

This is not to say that the change in state educational systems was unplanned. All of us can recall the statewide commissions, the mission statements, the Boards of Oversight created at every level. That these took serious account of our future resources, however, is far more open to doubt. In both education and health care the future was expected to take care of itself, and for many years it seemed to. Institutions were founded, grew, and became steadily more entrenched in our society, while the true trajectory of their costs as well as their ultimate purposes remained largely uncalculated.

The cultural texture of college and university life in the fifties was, like society at large, a curious amalgam. Those who had lived as adults through the Second World War wanted a society with as much stability and order as possible. The inevitable social changes brought about by the war itself were masked as far as possible. The fact that large numbers of women continued to work outside the home, for example, was concealed by a flood of film, music, and advertising oriented toward the coziest domesticity. The worries of Korea were somehow absorbed in a common sense optimism, which found its embodiment in General Eisenhower.

The colleges reflected these illusions in a texture of adolescent conventionalities, which led commentators to talk about these generations as "silent," without passionate social or political convictions. In truth their state of mind (so far as one can generalize) was as complex as that of their elders. Up to a point they enjoyed the comfortable ways of life, which their parents seemed to embody—or seemed to *want* to embody. At the same time there were undercurrents of force and conflict, which everyone, young and old, tried to keep under control. The profound and terrifying hope was that we could discipline the dragons of world conflict. That was the sound, so deep that we could not hear it but only feel it as a something, a vibration, a tremor in the earth. We gave it a phrase—the Cold War—but in fact it was Doomsday, the breath of annihilation, the hideous guest at the party.

Our reaching for security was so powerful that when supposedly comfortable Ike gave us one of the gravest and most prescient warnings any President ever articulated for his country, we could not handle it. We simply did not grasp what he was saying when he spoke of the military-industrial complex; we would be increasingly burdened and distorted for the next 30 years by the reality of that alliance; it drove us into false policies and deceits which are almost impossible to exaggerate. But in 1960 we did not understand, and we had no desire to ask, why Eisenhower pitched the danger exactly where we were told daily that our security lay. We were in the shadow of major social changes, and of policy commitments, which would alter the country's whole ethos, but at the national level we were unaware of it all. There was no daily presence to give substance to such a threat; it was to become one of the most abusive and corrupt alliances in our society.

The young, on the other hand, the college students of the later fifties, showed clearly their awareness of fear, high emotion, radical change. Their patterns were not yet fixed; certain sensitivities were as a result free to express themselves without conventional filters. To understand what was emerging we must think in metaphor—the metaphor of storm. Great oceanic disturbances send a signal ahead, a long swell, which has no relation to local weather conditions but only to the event which is still a thousand miles away. The student response to Kerouac's *On the Road* of 1956, their alertness to the unbridled energy of the early Presley and dozens of other voices in words and music began to show in increased restlessness about the unexamined norms of college life, and of personal life as well. Even without the cataclysmic events of the sixties there would have been major changes in student perceptions and in their social behavior. What students wanted was not clear in these years, but it was apparent that they wanted what they did not have. The familiar norms of social and sexual behavior were being called into question; the most solid early evidence of this came in the increased challenges to college regulations on the one hand and educational purposes on the other. Anyone close to students at that time can remember all too vividly the committee meetings, the student retreats, the issues (small in themselves) which multiplied endlessly the more one discussed them. By 1960 the student world—as much in the dark about the future as the rest of us—was already positioned for a dramatic response to the issues just ahead.

Often this complex excitement had a particularly painful quality for young faculty members. Many of them, like the students, had returned from the war to start or resume their careers. The pace of competition was extreme and the inevitable neurotic behavior created a super-heated atmosphere reminiscent of much that we read about in Vienna at the turn of the century. Unlike the *Fortune* fantasies one did not have to project these heady realities as a vision of the future; they added much to the immediate pressure of life and also to its opportunities.

I found this out in my first eighteen months of teaching, when I was given the chairmanship of the large sophomore course. This demanded the management of twenty or so of my fellow teachers. We stayed in some informal order and relationship through weekly "normal school" sessions to review the work under discussion. This was a first effort to help young faculty learn how to teach; the conduct of each session was given to a different member of the staff, and the rivalry among them was intense. One instructor was so painfully aware of this pressure that he kept echoing Othello at every fourth or fifth sentence, "Put up your knives," he would say as he advanced each new approach. No one laughed because everyone shared something of his edgy and threatened mood.

Chairing the course had obvious rewards and pitfalls for a neophyte. The knives might be put away in discussions among the others, but a good deal of stress was stored up for me. It was my first solid experience with envy and it put my precocity to the test. As one of my senior friends put it, "You're damned if you do, damned if you don't. They'll resent your management if it's vigorous but if it's gentle they'll cry out for leadership." All of this came duly to pass and was very good for me. I did the job for a second year, but meanwhile the strenuous times brought me another and more substantial adventure. One of the happier by-products of these double enrollment years was the opportunity to develop new courses. I was offered one in the European epic tra-dition (there were to be other courses in tragedy and comedy to round out this "new" idea of the so-called genre course, which would range across several cultures and languages). This was a bold departure from normal practice at the time and it allowed an absolutely major redirection of my intellectual life as well as my teaching career. I would take it with me in the years of altered duty and heavy administrative demand (it would always be there, as I told students in the 1960s, to keep me sane while the rest of the world was doing its best to destroy me). In today's language I was surfing; other aspects of the academic world—both those I saw and those I was still too naive to see—might pose problems in the future. But the teaching and research were an unclouded and intense daily pleasure, which also pushed me in new direc-tions.

This major development of my inner life in these years was the drawing together of my long-standing religious concerns and an emerging preoccupation with the bases of scientific thought. At one level this was the obvious question of faith and reason, but it took on some forms that were anything but routine. I had, furthermore, the impetus of the epic tradition in driving me toward some real effort to relate the two great modes of thought. One of the central characteristics of European epic is its drive toward the most basic issues of life; you cannot teach any one of the epics without confronting these issues, and their scope is such that you must meet them on their terms. You cannot choose to ignore the bedrock reality of each work; instead you must rise in your small way to meet it, and that demand in turn forces you toward your own articulations.

I was greatly helped by Whitehead and Collingwood, among others, as I set out to develop a mature understanding of scientif-ic thought—in both its power and its logical limits. Inevitably I had to deal with the issues of objective reality; objectivity in appraising a problem and its results became clear as a prime necessity in all scholarly and critical work. The other objectivity—that of dogmatic certainty about conclusions as well as *a priori* positions—emerged for me as a major limitation of thought, whether the issue was scientific, religious, or artistic. It had become a particular vexation in the sciences with their rapid ascent to power through their technological offspring. Dogma was all too easily turned into an absolute—a change that violated the very basis of the sciences as tentative, exploratory, subject to change in the face of new knowledge. The latest revelations of the Hubble telescope are a prime example, the recognition of sudden gene mutation an equally important shift in evolutionary thought. Years later, Richard Feynman would develop this awareness with the weight of his authority behind it; for me in 1950 it was a hard-won position.

It helped me greatly, not only in my grasp of the sciences but also in major revisions of my religious awareness. As a boy I had a thorough conventional training in my own Protestant tradition; it was highly useful now, as it merged with the great world-views of epic on the one hand, and my formal training in the uses of metaphor as well as symbolic structures of many kinds. These were great pathways of formal religious doctrine in many cultures, and through them I came to know a tentative, yet growing awareness of religious faith, which is a vigorous part of my life today. It has clearly developed in tandem with my still maturing awareness of scientific symbol, rhetoric and process. The latter is now a significant part of my professional work with optics, while its firm base lies in the work of my first teaching years.

The pleasure was heavily reinforced by the nature of the veterans who brought a special world with them. It was one of urgency, of eagerness and skepticism fused. It put up with no nonsense, and the Department had to suppress one notorious example. A young faculty member was one of that group of permanent graduate students who inhabit every great university. He was pressed into service when Yale, in deference to the veterans' enrollment, doubled the entering classes for four years. Worse, he happened to draw a freshman class almost totally made up of veterans; they put up with his extreme prosiness and uncertainty for six weeks; one fine Monday when he came in they stood up as a group, and the leader told him that they had a right to expect more than this. Then several of them picked him up, carried him outside in a gentle but firm way, and set him on his shaky legs outside the building.

They treated me to another form of testing, a bombardment of questions about legitimate matters but not those that concerned our work directly. I would thrust and parry in this swordplay of the mind, but we evolved a set of rules. They could bait me as vigorously as they wanted, but as soon as I said, "Ah, ha, that reminds me…" the game was over and they accepted the traditional rules of the class. Many were my elders, and by pushing me so hard they taught me how to teach.

They could not save me from mistakes that my other elders, the faculty, lured me into. When my mentor, Maynard Mack, was to be on leave for a year, I was asked to replace him in the big Shakespeare lecture course. There were, of course, issues of turf and seniority involved, and one senior professor exploded. "Damn it, why don't we just take a year off and just let him teach all of it?" The Chairman withdrew the suggestion, and I was relieved of an exciting piece of work (one for which I was certainly unprepared) and a distraction from the seminars in the epic tradition.

I have said that these seminars were made possible by the heavy enrollments; they were also a normal part of the residential colleges, and I taught mine in my office suite. The volume of applicants made two sections necessary—always fascinating from a technical viewpoint. The very contrast sharpened me in the questioning necessary to get life into the group. I remember well the class that was most silent and most stubborn, while it was also the most brilliant of all the groups. One day *I* exploded and accused them of indifference and myself of failure. They began to laugh (they were a group of seniors and very sure of themselves). "We know you," they said, "and we know that you'll wait for us to be forthcoming only so long. Then you'll give up, and we've decided to wait you out. We want to know what *you* think." How do you get around that? I told them what I thought. It was a vivid reminder of the limits of the Socratic method, with a group of students who were quite capable of turning it upside down and asking *me* the questions. It worked, of course; I held onto it as a warm reminder whenever I had to change an approach to the design of a class.

It might on the other hand be an individual book that forced a cluster of new teaching insights. We used *Emma* one year in the sophomore course—my idea, and a real source of heartburn for the staff. "Impossible to teach; young men in particular don't get Jane Austen; petty affairs in a smug village." This put me on my mettle, so that I took the tutoring session myself. I must put it on the record that twenty faculty members who don't want to teach are far worse than twenty undergraduates who don't want to learn. I teased out every social irony, explored the compelling qualities of this bright, outrageous young woman (whose lover virtually calls her by these epithets even as he proposes). There was one of those silences; I waited. "All right," said one of the best. "Yes, I see how it might go down that way. Now, will you come and teach it for me?" Under these many impacts my teaching became steadily more flexible, more alert to sudden shifts in the middle of a class, more wide-ranging without losing sight of the core of the subject. The scope of my work was varied almost from the start; the various styles I had developed to meet the demand would turn out to be central to future faculty-administration encounters.

And so was the scholarly work, that part of an academic's life for which the phrase "publish or perish" was created. This too, took on urgency in these years after the war; scholars back from service were in strenuous competition, and the economics of life (marriage and children during the war) made a pause for scholarly work doubly difficult. Many of course had been partway through graduate school so that they had a first hill to climb in order to get the degree before they could go on to further scholarship.

Inevitably the standards and true purposes of scholarship were put under pressure by this post war tangle of personal and professional demands. One of my much older colleagues at Yale said that he wanted to dedicate his first major work to "The little woman who made this book necessary." The jovial cynicism of his remark embodied a somber reality; scholarship which should result from one's best thought becomes, under pressure, a dues payment to the guild. In a curious echoing of the stages of graduate work, there is first an apprenticeship; after two or three years there is a journeyman period—and then if one is able, lucky, or both one becomes a Master Craftsman with permanent tenure. Here it is important to note again the medieval character of this career development and the virtual laying on of hands at every stage. There are, of course, sequences in medicine and law, steps of increasing responsibility, but none of them carries the ritual freight of one's career as a junior faculty member in a great university feels it. Life during these years is heavily conditioned by this one preoccupation.

As Yale handled the structure during my time, the critical passage was to the associate professor level and almost certain tenure. Before the War, this had taken ten years or more but now there was a good deal of external competition for the top group of young faculty so that the old-time pattern was considerably shortened. In my case the offer of an assistant professorship elsewhere brought me my first promotion after a year and a half of teaching. The five years just ahead would at least require that my dissertation become a book and that it receive some favorable notice. All of this was in the well-established pattern except that the tempo of events, the competition, and the very nature of the enterprise of higher education were all in ferment.

Above all, it was becoming clear in the late 1940s and early 1950s that the radical increase in post high school enrollment was not to be temporary. It was the shape of things to come and society itself was the driving force (for cultural and social as well as technical and economic reasons). A high school education was no longer enough. The dislocations of the war had changed everyone's aspirations even though the shift was most marked among minorities. The horizon of our expectations had been greatly extended just as our knowledge of European and Asian realities had expanded and deepened.

The most privileged of the private and public universities were not influenced by these pressures as abruptly as less established and therefore more fluid and responsive places. The young faculty in every place, however, felt these pressures; the mood created was both expansionist and edgy. My experience had all these emotional charges in it and something else. I had to prove myself in a setting which was my own. It is clear looking back that I was fighting for myself and for a position honestly earned rather than a reward for my skill at "Yaleing" as one of my students remarked to me. The political stresses were doubly rough because to those around me I had it made, while I was both fighting that perception and working strenuously to make my success come about. I was forcing myself. This did not destroy my great joy in every aspect of my work but it kept me from savoring or being at ease in the enjoyment.

Meanwhile, the great world was expanding its mammoth neuroses as a counterpoint to my petty ones. The aftermath of the War, the establishment of the United Nations, the aid plans for devastated countries, had elements of greatness and vision about them. The movement toward the cold war, on the other hand, was a step back into a world of fear and suspicion. The explosion of the first thermonuclear weapon confirmed the worst fantasies of a whole generation. It also put the rich culture of the continent into restraining boxes—boxes for thought and prisons for men. For the American universities, it meant the beginning of a great triple partnership—big science, big government and big universities that would reshape all three.

The fear of nuclear weaponry, and the Korean War with its explicit Chinese threat to world order, would set a tone of concern that in due course came to justify our intervention in southeast Asia. First, the universities would be preoccupied with the weaponry and the increasingly elaborate intelligence apparatus that supported it. Then would come the revolt of the young against both. The seed of the whole 60s turmoil was sown now, in the strange cross-current years between 1946 and the mid-50s—years of delayed hope and highly fantasized dreams of a 'normal' world that would in fact never exist again in the old ways.

My own pattern of life was much more private and domestic. In the academic mode three of us, all beginning faculty, had evenings of beer and Greek. We read the tragedians, as I remember, but with a rather comic attitude toward them and a complete and conscious rejection of the fact that we all had early classes the next morning. Much the same could be said for our student evenings at home, which were seminars in wallpaper removal and Saturday afternoon exercises in heavy construction. This welcome help came because my classes knew that Grace and I were repairing the cheapest house in greater New Haven, which we had been fortunate enough to find. There was no money for repairs, and students were a high-spirited part of what was, for me, my chief recreation during the seven years of my faculty time at Yale.

The rhythm of my life supported this focus for my energy. I have never had a talent for long hours at one task. By four o'clock every day I was ready to get on my bike and pedal the three miles home. In the evening I would prepare classes or correct papers. As I look back I am startled by the ease and joy of life, with secondhand clothes, a budget tight beyond present believing, and never a complaint between my wife and me. (She was a church historian's daughter and accustomed to living so austerely that, as she said, she and her slightly older sister had to share one doll between them as a Christmas present.) Each of us had a serious operation in these years, but that did not seem to dampen the upbeat tenor of life. (Obviously youth, small children and an opening career had a great deal to do with that.) It was a curious aspect of the Yale English Department at the time that virtually all of its members had independent incomes—some modest but some substantial indeed. (The standard joke elsewhere in the country was that at Yale men taught for love but married for money.) Maynard Mack and I were the two exceptions, but the mediocre salaries resulting from this departmental comfort level were a spur to us rather than a drag. We did not care to be told that salaries were low.because "the library alone is worth fifteen hundred a year" when our salaries were three thousand. We simply pushed harder to be the best professionals in the group.

Because the general temper of the time was so upbeat and yet so close to the years of war, it would serve as a benchmark from which to measure the supposedly quiet years between the early 50s and 1960. It would also turn into a nostalgic memory during the 60s to which it was in almost total counterpoint. Meanwhile I was beginning to move in a larger world without noticing its implications for my future. That may seem strange, but looking back it is clear that when the national experience first began to stir in my life it took the simple shape of a project and some deeply welcome additional income to be made. The offer came during a fellowship year in 1950–51, which allowed me to finish my first book, and was in itself a proof that the great world outside the universities was now inside them as well. The Korean War and the newly created Ford Foundation conspired in a singular way to give me a first exposure to the galaxy of colleges and universities that made up the pattern of American higher education. (It turned out to be a great corrective to Yale's golden provinciality.) There had been a sudden drop of enrollment since the start of that war and the Ford staff had the inspired idea of fellowships for senior faculty, which would in turn allow junior faculty to be retained who would otherwise have been furloughed. The Dean of Yale College was a major architect of the program, and he asked that I interview a large share of the candidates in the northeast. In doing this I traveled from Orono, Maine to Greencastle, Indiana and returned with appraisals of the 20 finalists in this area. Evidently my judgments stood up and the sudden enlargement of my horizon was a portent for the future. I did not consider it so at the moment, however, nor did I pay attention to the educational power structure that lay behind such programs (naive of me but quite true). I knew, however, that eight weeks at $200 a week was nearly half of my annual salary; I was perfectly clear about that.

The world of the foundations was in fact a relatively new one. There had been the various organizations created by Andrew Carnegie, members of the Mellon family and others. Now, however, came the first of the super-foundations, with great resources and equal zeal at putting them to work. Education was, almost by definition, a central concern from the start, and experiments tried at Ford would have a major impact on the work of dozens of other foundations in the future.

It is clear to me in hindsight that one of the administrative litmus tests for my future was my clear enjoyment of work like that in the Ford Faculty grant program. It was immediate, it was exciting, it was—to use an annoyingly apt cliché—real. So was the next unexpected demand that surfaced, though this one had a more familiar shape. The President's office called one morning to ask if I would serve as Executive Secretary of a Committee to review the educational programs in the Arts and Sciences. Whitney Griswold, the new President of Yale felt that it was time to go through this solemn ritual (which overtakes academic communities every generation or so). I was totally surprised to be asked but I felt, of course, that great things could be done. I would not realize for many years, however, that my peers were certain I had connived to get the job. (And forty years later I would smile as I read the summary of a similar Harvard study. A large part of each report could be exchanged with the other without any evidence of the switch.) Being thirty years old I worked at the project with great zeal and complete unawareness of what I was, in fact, learning: how people in the major different disciplines think about their fields of study, what their sacred icons are, what they will discuss freely and what on the other hand they assert as gospel. I gave up part of my teaching load to do this job, but no little bell rang inside to say, "This is dangerous knowledge, there's no telling where it might lead."

Yale like many other universities faced a faculty crisis in the early 1950s. Young faculty were being nominated for tenure level jobs three times as fast as their elders were retiring. This created a great bulge in the neck of the ostrich; it could not be quickly assimilated. I found myself in this position in 1952–53. I was approved for my associate professorship and then was told that the action must be delayed for a year or more. I had a good deal of company, I knew that I was young and, as a result, I was not troubled by the matter—particularly since I received most of the modest but badly needed salary increase that would go with the promotion. There was quite a stirring in the pigeon loft, however, and the Provost of the university as the chief academic officer was the center of the controversy. Once again there was a tiny action on my part that had consequences quite beyond my knowing. I felt that there was injustice in the criticism and I wrote the Provost, Ed Furness, to tell him that this particular assistant professor understood what and why. I did not mean to be cheeky or sycophantic; the letter was quite impulsive and was the only one

written by any of those affected. The Provost took it in the right
spirit and said so. He also told a few others about the letter, a small
matter which was somehow put together with the other and
much larger events in which I was embroiled. I did not know any
of this, naturally; nor did I know that my mentor, the Dean, had
already put his mark on my forehead and that mark quite simply
was, in the Dean's words, that "I was doomed to administration."
(This he told the full professors when they voted my second promotion.)

My individual experience at this critical moment does not by
itself deserve the attention given to it here; however, it implies and
illustrates much larger issues. Chief among them perhaps was the
assumption in the 1950s that administrators should be drawn
from the scholarly/teaching faculty and that this training was
essential if one were to do the administrative job properly. It was
not merely a question of membership in the guild, though that
was extremely important; it was a question of knowing what mattered, what was primary and what was not. One might call it a
highly developed instinct, of great value when one had to make
complex decisions without having time to work through the
whole equation.

The second issue is that of the *mode* of selection. The choosing of college and university presidents has always been a complex
job, and though the criteria have changed, the process is as vexing today as it was forty-five years ago. Several major constituen-
cies are involved—the same ones that often make life hell for the
president after he has been appointed. When these groups have
pooled all their requirements a wonderfully unrealistic profile
emerges; it is reported that the senior Fellow of the Yale
Corporation said at one point, "Yes, yes, this is all very well, but
is Christ a Yale man?" In such confusion there has always been
room for organizations as well as individuals to serve as informal
clearinghouses. The Carnegie Corporation served this way for
many years and several other foundations are currently doing the
same thing—even though the formal recruiting process is far
more structured now than in the 1950s.

The definition of the position—indeed its total function—has
changed markedly in the last forty-five years. It will be a bench-

mark for describing the major changes that have come about in the college and university world. For the moment it is enough to say that I suddenly found myself pondering this subject of the Presidency in an intimate way; I was astonished to be in such a predicament. It had never entered my mind, though I found that no one believed me. I had sensed that I might be in line for a college Mastership; but beyond that my world of teaching and scholarship was, I believed, completely satisfying, and I knew nothing about that mark of Cain—the cloud no bigger than a man's hand which my mentor Dean DeVane was already turning into a whirlwind.

THE NEUTRAL AIR

Who stole the gay charisma I once had
(Or thought I had; it hardly matters now)?
The glass of time was sunlight, days were gold,
And all my chatter shone with assurances;
In that god-guarded playground of the self
I lit a hundred flames to match my dreams.

Now at the plane window I see my image—
No wreath, no statue, but fifteen hundred feet
A minute of climb through the gray blanket of my years.
The single sun has shared my abdication,
And casually absorbed my self-esteem.

CHAPTER THREE:
The Lawrence Years

Sleigh Ride
1953–1963

It started as the academic year was starting—New Haven, late September: golden and busy with the most familiar fall chores. Suddenly the phone in my Saybrook College Office: "You don't know me; my name is David Stevens, and I want to talk with you about coming to Lawrence College as President now that Nathan Pusey has gone to Harvard. I'll be there in forty-five minutes." Nothing more. This was an obvious hoax, but as a courtesy to the gods I would see if I could possibly identify this man Stevens. Lo and behold: there he was. Lawrence Trustee, retired Director of the Humanities for the Rockefeller Foundation, and a good deal more. Forty-five minutes later he was at the door, as advertised; we talked for three hours, and at the end David Stevens said, "Why don't you come back with me?" It was strange to counsel prudence to this mogul, but I did. "Your friends will be sure I'm pushing myself; besides, we need to draw a deep breath and think about this." "You'll hear from us," and he was gone, leaving behind him a strong sense of fantasy. David Stevens might be real; nothing else was.

That fall was unusually busy: the Committee on the Liberal Arts was winding up, and I had the final report to write. Then, exactly three weeks later, a Monday telegram: "Suggest you fly out for visit Wednesday or preferably tomorrow. G. Banta, Chairman, Lawrence Trustee Committee." Much scrambling and Grace with a bad cold; Wednesday afternoon we were off on a storybook adventure, no matter what came of it. Assistant Professors at thirty-two do not include this kind of visit among their options.

As an introduction to a new world the trip itself was remarkable. The last stage of the journey, from Milwaukee to fabled Oshkosh was by DC-3, an equally fabled plane. Aboard was an old man just back from some kind of contract work for the big air base in Thule; his talk about what he had done in the Arctic lent a sense that we too were going to the border of the world. Friendly strangers in the dim light of a Quonset hut arrival building and then a fifteen-mile drive to Neenah, another Indian name. (Amusingly enough, the town turned out to be one of the three wealthiest in the United States; the other two were small towns in Connecticut.)

For the next day and a half it was all Lawrence and Appleton; the latter sounded bucolic but was the family name of Amos Lawrence's wife. We found ourselves back in our own New England past, but only as a backdrop to the present and hoped-for future, which we discussed with dozens of faculty, trustees and students. To this day the visit is a blur, but a remarkably comfortable and honest blur, in no way stuffy or pretentious. The few awkward moments were minimized by the willingness of our new friends to ease us over our ignorance. One of these moments was a ride with George Banta. We were suddenly passing by a huge, brightly lit factory almost jumping with some kind of heavy machinery in full operation. "What is *that?*" "One of our factories." "Why so late?" "Well, you see, it doesn't pay to run these long-run presses much less than twenty-four hours a day." "Sorry, I didn't realize the volume of your printing." "I should have explained; we publish 110 learned journals, most of the country's fraternity and sorority magazines, and three quarters of the work-books used in the public schools of the country." I silently digested the fact that in many ways this spot was more active and alert than New Haven. George Banta took great pleasure in arranging such exercises in my education.

After our introduction to the college and its regional community we climbed back aboard the DC-3 and gathered up the strands of our daily life. It would be foolish to say that nothing had changed, but certainly nothing further was said; the trip slipped back into fantasy for another three weeks. Then, on a soft late October evening came the call, and I realized how I had hoped for it. "Will you accept?" "Yes." "Then the Committee must come to visit you." I was embarrassed at that, since I already knew who they were, and I was left with the further need to keep security for two weeks.

Grace and I sat on the front steps of our old house and tried to anticipate the changes that were to follow these quiet moments. We could not explain why we were so willing to go, to give up an assured future in a great university for the major demands and expectations we could already picture—even in our ignorance. We had truly been attracted to that new world, but we were *ready* to be attracted; and that was a surprise to us. I knew why the Lawrence community had taken to Grace; I have never been able to understand their acceptance of me, but I felt a strong urge to do the job ahead, and a good deal of confidence that I could manage it. I would have to assume that my mentor Bill DeVane was right when he pronounced me "doomed to administration."

There was nothing superficially right about the visit that my new friends insisted on making. Just as they walked into the office I received my copy of the *Yale Daily News* with its two-inch headline: *Yale Faculty Member to Succeed Nathan Pusey.* I said to myself, "This affair is over before it begins," and I spread the paper out on my desk. I didn't have time to apologize; the

Chairman of the committee—George Banta again—began to smile a great, satisfied smile. "Well, well, I didn't think mighty Yale would care about a little Wisconsin college. *You,*" he said, poking me in the chest and still laughing, "call the Dean at Lawrence right now. We'll break the story ourselves this afternoon even though the full Board hasn't voted yet." This was my first encounter with crisis management, and it took a few days to track the security leak—our small son had a nursery school teacher who was also the wife of a junior faculty colleague.

We talked over many important things with our new friends but (as they reminded me later) no one brought up the matter of salary at all. We were amused at ourselves and took it as a very good omen; my starting salary was to be $11,000 per year, twice that of my salary at Yale. The detail of this personal, thoroughly non-legalistic transaction is important because it sheds some light on the college world as it was at that time. It stands in total contrast to the disquieting economic and corporate patterns in the present university structure, which have developed over the years. The Lawrence side of it, which I did *not* know at the time, is equally illuminating. I was the innocent in the drama; the real participants were all about me, but invisible. I was aware only of Dean DeVane's vision of my future. Enter David Stevens, calling him; "One question before you think: who ought to be the next president of Lawrence? Douglas Knight? Thank you and goodbye." He asked the same question in the same abrupt way of three others and then called me directly. DeVane was asked to go one step further and write a note about the candidate (as I had suddenly become). Senior trustees at Lawrence were thunderstruck (their word to me), when, instead of the expected formal note of endorsement, they received a seven-page handwritten letter, the detail of which I was never allowed to see. There were also opinions from two former Presidents of Lawrence, (Wriston and Pusey), and from older contemporaries like Vic Butterfield, the President of Connecticut Wesleyan. There was some careful scouting, but nothing to mitigate or lessen the responsibility the Trustees assumed in offering the job to a young, inexperienced and publicly unknown academic. I would know many Boards in the next forty years, but never anything to equal this one for its ease, self-confidence and total lack of self-importance.

With all this, the Trustees were extremely well informed about the appropriate part they should play in the affairs of the college. This had been put to the test just after I arrived in a way that brought the public world into a tense encounter with the private world of the college. Senator McCarthy had been born near Appleton, and Appleton was to be his earliest political power base. He had fanatical support from the right wing of the Republican Party in the state, of course, and the split between extreme and moderate Republicans had carried directly into the Board of Trustees. Naturally I was as green as grass, as my grandfather would have said, when it came to these divisions. My own political exposure had been to the moderate wing of the Democratic Party: I was a typical young academic in my thinking about these matters and had no intimate knowledge of Senator McCarthy's savage games.

My education began quickly. *Life* came to Appleton the week of my Installation, to do a piece on the Senator's hometown. Though I was quite incidental to that story, I was photographed with a quotation—"I'm not in politics; I have a job to learn."—I heard a few remarks from Yale friends about my rapid loss of backbone, and eventually I remembered that I *had* made that statement. It was in response to a *Time* reporter who had asked if I planned to go into Wisconsin politics. I found myself getting lessons—triple lessons—about the real freedom of the press to control the text, about McCarthy's true viciousness, and at the same time about the gullibility of my Yale friends.

The pro-McCarthy hysteria was like nothing I ever met— then or afterwards. After I invited a highly articulate Republican Alderman to speak about local government, I found myself personally attacked as though I had invited the head of the KGB for an honorary degree. The partisan anger was beyond credence. The public lack of balance took longer to right itself; when the city woke one May Day to find a hammer and sickle flying at the top of the college's new FM radio tower, there were serious cries for a political investigation. If the outraged ones had known who actually had put the flag there I would have had a major charge of college radicalism on my hands. A team of two had managed to climb the 110 feet without killing themselves (or I might have had to deal with manslaughter as well): one was the eldest son of my Lawrence predecessor, the President of Harvard; the other the only son of the senior professor in Lawrence's English Department, Warren Beck. Looking back, the prank was naive and somehow touching; at that moment it was a litmus test for political insanity. In any case, I had told the truth when I said I had a job to learn.

The American college is a remarkable institution, and in the 1950s a college president held a most unusual position—in the community, in the college itself, and within an educational community in some ways regional, in others quite national in its impact. My constituency—students, faculty, trustees, alumni and the community affected by the college—were rarely synchronous in their desires and dislikes. I would ignore any of them at my peril, and yet I had to be strong enough to think for myself as I planned for the future of the place. Fortunately for me the trustees had had a good deal of practice in educating presidents; they actually seemed to enjoy the job. In addition to Presidents Wriston and Pusey, a number of Deans had also gone on to senior positions elsewhere; this was one of the ways in which Lawrence felt it had a significant part to play in the national educational enterprise. The trustees seemed optimistic that this tradition could continue, an attitude of which I was at the moment unaware. Even if I had been aware of it, it was my task to walk into my new responsibility at half time, and to bring the year to a successful conclusion while I set about learning what the job was. It would be more accurate, however, to say that I opened my eyes and my mind so that the job itself could show me what I needed to do. This was the opposite of a passive encounter; every visitor, every phone call demanded action, and at a pace I had never known or imagined. I did not even know enough to realize that this way of learning such a job was the only feasible one; in fact the work was so multiple that any abstract discussion of it would be fatuous and false to the reality.

The college presidency of the 1950s was, much as it had always been, a position of considerable authority and responsibility, with very little staff support. (Proliferation of staff began in the

1960s and raises important questions of educational management structure today.) I found myself chairman of the faculty, senior budget officer, public relations expert, staff recruiter, student advisor, public speaker *ad nauseam,* and janitor when necessary. The job turned out to be intensely exciting, and so lively that I had no time to ask—like the centipede—which leg came after which.

Presidents are supposed to have road maps for their institutions. I developed my plan from inside. First, I was young and ignorant, and asking questions was the only reasonable way to work. Second, early on I discovered a bundle of urgent needs, and my program was thereby quickly defined. Five major examples of need come to mind today as fresh as they were in February 1954, when we arrived at Lawrence: library, salaries, staff (especially in the sciences), the physical plant and educational endowments. Preparations for obtaining a possible Ford grant put great pressure on all of us in the college to project our long-term needs, and one driving force emerged from our work: competition with other colleges of our general pattern. Even without Ford we would have been addressing our major weaknesses. Lawrence was poor; but its reputation went far beyond its modest resources, and its five major areas of weakness needed attention simultaneously. If one wanted a sharply defined program, here it was. It was not boldly innovative; it assumed that we were clear about the nature of a fine liberal education and that we were unremitting in our determination to find resources for it—and as a corollary to enhance our public reputation in every constructive way.

The college needed to continue the tradition of its strong past leadership. Henry Wriston, truly one of my great mentors, had defined Lawrence's major purposes and direction; it was my job to secure the means for getting there. Given the reverence for libraries that had always been a part of my life, I was as much concerned to increase its purchasing budget as to increase faculty salaries. I had my first great awakening when the librarian said very crisply, "We don't need more money; I can't read all the books we order right now." He wasn't kidding, but he accepted the changes that were in progress and we got on well. I was determined to augment the old Carnegie Library, and the addition remains today as a modest service building for the great new library.

There was much agitation about faculty salaries in the mid 1950s. The AAUP had taken upon itself the task of ranking institutions, and Lawrence was not doing well in comparison to the colleges with which we liked to compare ourselves. We had raises every year, and by 1963 could justly say that, though we still lacked many things, we had put the salary scale on a sound footing. This in turn helped immensely in attracting and retaining strong faculty, particularly in the sciences where matters had been neglected. One always builds in a new hope with each improvement, of course, and the gift of the Youngchild Science Center would become our much needed and appreciated reward for having greatly expanded our efforts in the areas of teaching and research.

Each development in the physical plant was a direct response to student needs in housing, laboratories and the like. We had no problem in identifying our needs, just in paying for them. As the future history of the college would show, the creation of a proper alumni program played a great part in meeting these needs as it did in strengthening every other aspect of the college. The Ford Program (which I will discuss in detail) together with the alumni's heightened awareness, played a major role in meeting our needs for endowment, which in 1953 was only slightly larger than the operating budget—a perilous position. Our programs and priorities during my time as President all revolved around this bundle of urgent needs. The education we were able to offer at the end of the decade was substantially better than at the start; I have looked on that fact as my major contribution to Lawrence—that and, of course, the enhanced continuing level of support which we were able to put in place.

My work at Lawrence was greatly influenced in pace and extent by the nature of the 1950s, which built its updraft of optimism on the euphoria of the immediate postwar years. At the same time a subtle change was beginning to show itself in the students. They were far more questioning and uncomfortable about our world than their elders realized; it would take me several years to perceive this new reality. Meanwhile I found these students appealing, more naive in style than those I had taught at Yale but equally stimulating in class. (I taught the European Epic course as well as several others at Lawrence and later at Duke.)

There was a humorous cast in much of my early experience at Lawrence. My new trustee and administrative friends protected me as I met the routines and deadlines that dictated so much of my daily life. When it came to the budget, however, no one could save me from the anguish of a $50,000 shortfall that looked, in the context of my previous life, both irresponsible and enormous. The salary increases that I knew we must have stood out like an orange stuck in the neck of the ostrich. In fear and trembling I went to the May meeting of the Trustee Executive Committee. The Chairman was a hard-bitten lawyer, President of Kimberly Clark, whose gravel voice could turn "Good morning!" into a challenge. After I had outlined the budget there was a slight pause. "You've heard the President's recommendations; is there a motion to approve?" Indeed there was, and thirty seconds later we had a budget, deficit and all. "But I've been worrying about it for two weeks," I blurted out, "and you pass it like that!" Well, Douglas," said the Chairman, "do you want us to pass it again?" That broke up the meeting and liberated me.

Of all the constituents I had to serve and (if possible) to lead, the faculty were the most complex, the most unrelenting and at the same time the most changeable in their views. I had a good introduction at Yale to these distempers of the mind, but it was quite a different matter when I was both moderator and target. (At Lawrence the President chaired all faculty meetings.) I quickly learned that faculty dissent was a favorite parlor game—but I never could play it as casually as it often deserved. The most difficult aspect of faculty relationships lay in the almost consistent negativism of a minority who were as difficult with their colleagues as they were with me. It was just as well that I did not know what lay ahead in the 90s, when a mean-spirited doctrinaire mood would almost come to seem the standard stance taken in any subject of academic discourse. In the 1950s I was able to find in a majority of cases a consensus of opinion, which was my customary goal. (I had read about the Robert Hutchins method of politicizing for votes, but I never felt comfortable with that. I knew, too, that many surface achievements were eventually reversed in reaction against his years at Chicago.)

Students were the wonderful, mercurial center of the enterprise, and in many ways I saw them more clearly than I had at Yale. One obvious reason for this was my immediate involvement in finding and interesting them in Lawrence. There was something innocent and festive about the prospective student evenings; I realized that I was making a sales pitch for a place I believed in; I realized also that I made light of its deficiencies and built up its virtues. The curious truth, however, was that I was listening, myself, to the song I was singing; and I was excited by it. A major result of this manner of recruitment was a community of interest after these young people came to Lawrence. I found that somehow I had time to be concerned over them, to rejoice in their festivals and rituals and to lend active support to the attitudes and values I was trying to get them to accept. (Later I would look back at my early years at Lawrence in wonder that these student relationships could have been so idyllic and so intimate.)

A larger world of action and preoccupation took hold of me within a very few years. This was in good part the result of certain energies loose in the world of the later1950s, and also in good part the result of my own personal clock, which was set at the right time to involve me with certain events. I was visible to a degree and had not yet been "committeed" to death. To my ingenuous mind these new demands were exciting—brave new worlds. The movement toward increased industry support for private colleges was just getting underway in part as a countervailing force against the newly established public colleges. New foundations were also being created with a major focus on higher education; urgent questions were being asked about the preparation of teachers; there was more specialized concern about the preparation of college administrators; a network of threats and obligations was evolving from the cold war and the scientific/technical competition with the USSR. As a preface to relating my specific encounters I should say that the common view of the fifties as a time of hyper-normality and retreat to conventional pre-war values is simply not borne out by the facts. The issues that I have just sketched are only samples of those that defined higher education in the period; so much was initiated and expanded. A time of doubt and criticism would emerge only later, with the complex upheavals of the 1960s. My personal encounter with all of this began when I participated in a seminar at the Harvard Business School, which brought its famous case study method to bear on a carefully developed group of academic problems. These sessions were highly effective, as were many of the associations that developed among the twenty or twenty-five couples who were invited to attend. Above all, they created an attitude toward problem-solving which was the ideal prelude to the needs of the decade ahead.

That decade of the 1950s reconciled to a high degree for me the demands of the inner needs of the college and the larger demands of the country. This must have been true for many other Presidents as well, but I certainly found that a surprising number of the external demands sooner or later shed light on the obligations right at home. The National Commission on Accreditation, for example, had a subsection with the fine acronym of NCATE—the National Commission for the Advancement of Teacher Education. A subsection of this group had the thorny job of reconciling the views on course requirements held by the professional educators on the one hand and the liberal arts colleges on the other. Since I found myself chairing this circus I had an intimate look at one of the questions still vibrating today. Who has the power to set standards in a particular field? Every one agrees that they should exist, but there are fearful arguments over *what, who* and *why*. Lawrence prepared quite a few teachers but was determined to keep the formal education courses to a minimum; in the end, the argument for flexible and minimal requirements prevailed.

The window opened—one might say at the other end of the building—when the Woodrow Wilson graduate fellowships were endowed by two major grants from the Ford Foundation. As a Charter Trustee of the Woodrow Wilson Foundation I found that our task was to oversee this major national program for graduate fellowship support in the humanities and social sciences. The impact of heavy government subsidy was already being felt in the sciences, and the Wilsons were seen as a counterbalance. Their impact would be felt for thirty years after the decade of the actual program, because the selection process was so effective in maintaining high traditional standards for a generation of scholars, teachers and administrators. This encounter with a major national program opened my mind to the great diversity of higher education as it was being shaped in the 1950s, and equally it sharpened my perception of the qualities I needed to seek out in the hiring of new faculty for Lawrence.

My insight was extended in many other ways—by remarkable collegiate gatherings like the one at Cyrus Eaton's Pugwash retreat center; by the Hazen Foundation Board as a revelation of how a small organization might stimulate the mind and spirit; by the American Assembly meeting of 1960 which produced under my editorship the first study of the federal government and higher education; and finally, of course, by the major Special Grants program of the Ford Foundation. The sum of all of these encounters was deeply significant for me; each committee, each meeting had its base in some aspect of the national ferment in education, and it had two other dimensions of meaning as well.

First, these involvements had value for Lawrence and were in some way a path to strengthening the college's position. Second, they were for me personally an education far greater than I perceived at the time. I was being trained to think of the educator's job as multiple and intensely active, embracing many aspects of our society and inevitably raising basic questions as to the direction to be taken both by society and by the formal educational systems where my life and career lay.

The emerging picture was not clear to me at the time because of the many immediate demands I was responding to and because something strange, stressful and ultimately disruptive was happening to the country at large. Our country was in a better position than any other to rejoice at the end of the Second World War. Precisely for this reason, when we fell into the Cold War anxiety was intensified and then further deepened by the fusion of military ambition and a serious ignorance of the true policy directions of the USSR. Ambassador Anatoly Dobrynin's remarkable memoirs reveal the depth of Russia's desire to avoid confrontation with the United States—a desire frustrated by America's stance as we developed more and more sophisticated interactions among our universities, the military and industry.

My ignorance about this growing anxiety was as great as any-one else's, but I can cite one chilling glimpse that I caught of it in the winter of 1960. I was in New Delhi briefly, following a SEATO meeting in Karachi. Plane schedules on the new jets were erratic, and I was held over for half a day before leaving for home via Bangkok. When I finally set out from my hotel I found that I was sharing the car with a Russian couple and their five-year-old son. Remembering my own four boys at home, I made some ami-able remark about the boy, to which his father gave an unexpect-ed reply. "Are you Canadian?" "No, American." They were seat-ed in front of me, and I could see their body language. The woman actually drew the little boy close, as though the whole menace of the United States was in the car with them. It was a terrible moment in a dark time, and my totally spontaneous response was, "We're here together; no one can hear us. I don't know how we're going to manage it, but we must not allow our-selves to be trapped in some violent encounter." Her face when she turned to me was white, twisted. "You Americans are so for-tunate; do you know how many Russians died in the recent war? Twenty-five million." Then we talked together about what could be done; it turned out that the man was the Pravda Indian Bureau Chief, and there was no doubt that their fear was as real as my own. It would take thirty-five years, however, before I got a full view of the Russian policy position from Dobrynin; in 1960 I dis-covered only that while we were indeed very far apart we were even closer together.

Many years later when I was able to reflect further on that period, I saw in depth how far from the truth the conventional view of the 1950s "normality" was and the extent to which any simplistic view of the period could only be trivial and inaccurate. At the same time there was a great reluctance in society at large to confront its newly evolving role. Comfortable Grandfather Ike was far more reassuring than any cold war analysis (even though he gave us our clearest warning of trouble ahead).

Many specific difficulties had emerged by 1960, and their full force would show itself in the decade ahead. They were a constant concern for me, believing as I did that the college *community* was essential if liberal learning were to have any lasting presence in our society. At the same time my own position was becoming steadily more complex in relation to that community. By 1960 I was involved in a dozen national organizations that defined the major concerns for higher education. I was invited to participate in these organizations in part, as I well knew, for totemic reasons, as a midwestern liberal arts college head; and in part because of my genuine desire to learn at first hand about the major issues. In my early years at Lawrence I saw these organizations as relevant to the development of the college; now I was seeing their intrinsic and far-ranging value.

A word about the new foundations will make clear their importance in the 1950s. The history of charitable foundations is long, honorable and—except for religious and academic establishments in Europe and the royally founded schools in the Middle and Far East—is largely a United States creation. Before the tax structure made them almost obligatory there were already a fair number in existence; Andrew Carnegie's comment that, "he who dies wealthy dies disgraced," underlay some of the early giving, which in its motivation went back to early Calvinist and colonial days. Service to the community was vital in the early establishment of colleges in New England and—most strikingly—along the moving frontier. The secular foundations, as one might call them, sprang into great numerical prominence only after the Second World War, however, in a movement to protect and perpetuate the great resources which could still be generated in a single lifetime—as the Packard and Doris Duke Foundations have recently shown us.

My encounters with that special world of giving began with my early teaching and continued in a variety of ways throughout my academic life and beyond. Two carried particular weight for me and will suggest the stimulus to both thought and action, which, as a group, they nurture. With the first, the Woodrow Wilson National Fellowship Foundation, I enjoyed the privilege of Trusteeship from its formal beginning in 1957 until my retirement as Chairman in 1994. With the second, the Ford Foundation (which brought the Woodrow Wilson Foundation into being) I participated in several grants awarded to the institutions I headed.

The Ford Foundation, particularly in its freewheeling early years, had major implications for education at all levels. Its resources were uniquely large, and it partook of the postwar euphoria in which all problems seemed soluble as soon as articulated. It emerged quickly as a complex Foundation in its operation; it supported outside projects, while at the same time it administered programs developed by its own staff. (And it seemed uncomfortable at times with the dichotomy, as though it were torn between the talents of its society and the desire for kudos on the part of its corporate ego.)

I would not have made such a criticism in the 50s and 60s. I was as dazzled as those around me by the achievements which some of the large grants made possible. The Woodrow Wilson program had started at Princeton in response to the war, which put immense pressure on young men to choose careers with more immediate rewards than college teaching offered. It ran along on a very modest basis, piecing together support from several sources, which provided up to two hundred graduate fellowships a year by the mid–1950s. Vice President Clarence Faust at Ford responded to the program, both for what it had already achieved and for what he perceived to be a major future need for college faculty in the humanities and social sciences. He proposed a support level that would provide more than a thousand fellowships a year for five years—a grant renewable for a second five-year period. A much more formal structure was demanded of such a foundation, and I found myself among its charter trustees.

The Woodrow Wilson appointment was the beginning of a thirty-seven year involvement with the Foundation, in the last eleven of which I served as Chairman. I was matured by this relationship more than by any of the other committees and commissions which were part of my almost daily routine. My interest was first captured by the straightforward importance of the program. (Thirty years later I thought it somewhat *too* single-minded in the context of the strenuous educational demands that were by then upon us.) I was greatly intrigued by the operation itself, which depended for its success on very substantial volunteer work from

more than one hundred-twenty regional committee members.
These passed their recommendations to one national committee;
the total program was managed by a very small central staff with
its only two functions: to guarantee the high quality of the selection process and to give all possible attention to the progress of the
recipients.

Perhaps the program meant so much to me because its later
development resonated so well with my own. After eleven years
Ford decided both that the major work had been done and that
the Woodrow Wilson Foundation was not fully responsive to the
needs which had emerged during the late 1960s. By that time my
own professional world had been disrupted—indeed destroyed—
and the new demands put upon Woodrow Wilson and myself
would bind us closely together. At a time when my orbit took me
far from my professional past, Woodrow Wilson continued to give
me a perspective on the educational world which I would value
even while I fought against it as too simple and even timid.

Meanwhile I found myself coping with a far more immediate
example of the power of the Foundation world. In the early
1950s the senior people at the Ford Foundation cast a searching
eye at the private universities of the country and saw weaknesses
there which were in fact analogous to those which led to their
handsome support of the Woodrow Wilson Foundation. An
imbalance between the public and private universities was emerging as a result of the heavy postwar support of the state university and college systems. (In time I would become an intimate
friend of the program's developer and administrator so that I was
allowed to see its larger purpose.) The original plan had been to
give massive support to a few universities that were 'on the brink
of greatness', and so move them toward a new level of excellence.
From the beginning there was a matching feature tailored to the
fund-raising capability of the institution. Stanford was a prime
example of this first phase: twenty-five million dollars, to be
matched three to one. This was an enormous effort for the period, and it succeeded just as Ford hoped. Stanford owes its
remarkable development in part to this high expectation, based
firmly on the major Ford gift.

As the university grants took hold it became clear that the liberal arts colleges faced many of the same pressures of competition which were nipping at the universities, and so the college gifts program was developed along the same lines: exhaustive presentation of the college's financial and educational plans, detailed analysis of the uses to which a grant would be put, and a formula for matching designed to stretch each place to its limit.

Lawrence was in the second group of colleges to receive support. Years later I would learn that by the time a college was invited to submit its proposals the basic decision in its favor had already been made. Certainly this reality was well masked during the process; I felt that I was as much on trial as a young faculty member. The projections required a great deal of searching—and useful—analysis of every aspect of the college's life, with the purpose of making certain that its projected financial position had some rational basis. By the time a grant was made, the institution was well prepared to make wise use of it.

That discipline was—and is still—a crucial element in college and university operation. Taken superficially, it seems so obvious as to need no comment. Reality is quite the opposite; institutions are always tempted by money (which may well be given for some marginal purpose and short-term effect) that may, over the long run, involve heavy and unexpected continuing commitments. I saw little of this in 1957, but I was indecently well pleased to have the grant, which did in fact give Lawrence a jump in resources quite unlike anything in its previous history. Support continued at a much higher level than in the years before the grant, and the level of achievement in every aspect of college life was greatly enhanced.

Many years later, after the Duke years, which also included Ford matching, I did a modest study of the impact of these grants. The results were remarkable in virtually every case, and they went quite beyond the direct impact of the dollars involved. It is ironic in the extreme that the Ford Foundation itself decided that the program had not been particularly effective. I could not avoid the conclusion that Ford felt critical precisely because of its success, in which the Foundation's role was quite passive. The major accomplishments should have been measured by the cumulative achievements of the individual places, not by the mere financial massiveness of the program. Perhaps the great foundations fail at times to recognize their own pioneering work: they are bell-wethers without realizing it. And perhaps it is not their kind of achievement.

It may seem that, on the personal level, with so much urgency and intensity on the professional level both in advancing the position of the college and dealing with major national issues, there would be little room for me to enjoy the fun of things like the eccentricity of faculty and trustees or the excitement of finding able new recruits for the faculty. As I look back, however, there seems to have been time to rejoice in the excitement of all of it, and time to enjoy that texture of activity in all its richness. For me as for others such was the temper of the college.

There were several reasons for this for me personally, and they came together to form a point in time, a golden few years in which everything seemed to work. There was my youth; my very inexperience made every day exciting, and even the baiting tactics of equally young faculty members did not destroy the thrill of a new course, an approved program, a better schedule. There was the simplicity of the administrative structure, which allowed problems to be met intimately and immediately. There was the chance for much direct student interaction in dealing with significant issues—some of which were of course not significant at all. There was college athletics as it should be, without the gladiators and the money. (One did not have to ask what percentage of the athletes graduated; they were *all* expected to graduate while on the other hand their achievements had a value for the college and received a degree of attention which no hired hands could ever have matched.)

The size of the place allowed working intimacies of every sort—often evolving into increasingly close friendships. Alumni meetings or prospective student receptions can be heavy going, but if one knows the college group attending there is immediately a core of social warmth that makes the awkwardness melt away. Each meeting builds on the ones before it, and though it seems trite to say so I found the sense of community to be so alive that one could almost touch it. For exactly the same reason, of course, the abrasive or conflicted events were direct, intimate, and demanded immediate action. They could not be temporized or committeed to limbo; that is a trick for the large places.

I shall never forget, for example, one particular morning of a spring meeting of the Board, which always included the faculty promotions and appointments list. Two hours before the meeting a senior professor called to ask for the review of a brilliant young teacher who was up for tenure. When I demurred, my colleague simply said, "Ask him about that Ph.D. which he lists in the catalogue." This question was like a dead fish at a garden party, but there was no help for it. When questioned, the faculty member quickly responded, "No, I don't have the degree; when I was appointed I told Nate Pusey that I would receive it before I came here in the fall, but I was working on another paper and didn't complete the degree; and when it was published in the catalogue I was too embarrassed to say anything." The monograph had in fact become an interesting first book. My response was immediate: "Look, it was foolish to leave it there, and you know how some of your colleagues would act if they knew about it. I'll keep your name on the list for promotion because you deserve it, but you have to protect me by getting that damned dissertation finished this summer. No excuse and no delay. I'll try to square it with the one man who knows." This last was not a comfortable job, but more than forty-two years later the faculty member was still hard at it, still a splendid teacher. I had violated the letter of the law, but certainly not the spirit.

That direct confrontation worked out, but what about the paranoid psychologist who had to be dismissed and gave all his students disastrous grades which he challenged the Dean to change? Or the faculty member who set out to pick apart the Chairman of his Department? And there was an Assistant Dean of Women who discovered that her superior was a crypto-Lesbian, and worked diligently to destroy her. In cases like these there was a uniquely sharp edge to decisions that only a small community could create.

Above all, there were singular pleasures, some ethical, some financial, some personal, which flowered in this setting. The admission of the first black students since the 1920s led to one of those confrontations that seem scripted for a grade B movie. Two anguished senior Trustees (I never could fathom their intense passion for the fraternity cause) came in protest to acknowledge that the admission was upheld by the courts, but, "Why here and why now?" I, and a third Trustee who had come along "to make sure they don't try to run over you," simply sat in silence; the two made their pitch again, were faced with more silence and finally stood up and left. I realized that they had come under orders from the national office. I knew also that they published most of the fraternity house organs; silence was the only effective answer, and they took it away with them.

Fruitful in quite another way was the afternoon spent with an old gentleman who had started work in a paper mill when he was twelve and wound up as Director of Forest Operations for the same major company. He came back to Appleton in his retirement, and let it be known that he had some interest in the college. He was not prepossessing, his suit was quite ordinary and his voice was rasping; but he asked the question that set a benchmark for all my future fundraising. "Tell me, young man, what would do your college more good—half a million dollars or a million?" Later the nettled comment of his lawyer to me, as we were leaving, was, "I can't imagine why Cap said that to you; he knew perfectly well what he planned to do." That was a lawyerly remark; matters should be tidy. But I knew why; for a million dollars the donor is entitled to a little fun.

I have offered these disparate examples of certain social elements of life as I personally experienced it in a liberal arts college to illustrate the varied humanity and constant 'aliveness' of such a place. The inner character of the education offered there is another and far more complex matter, for which the social fabric is only an essential introduction and companion.

I rejoiced in the texture of that life, while I was steadily involved in defining some national understanding of liberal learning. I was asked to speak to this very subject when the Rockefeller Institute decided to formalize its emergence as a great international graduate school in the sciences. The celebration reached back to the University of Padua as a 12th century counterpart of the Institute's new dignity, but there was a sense of the whole continuity of higher education throughout the speeches and rituals. I found that my own role at this event had a particular significance, a unique one indeed, since a high percentage of the graduate student body at Rockefeller came from a liberal arts undergraduate background.

My convictions about liberal education reached a high level of coherence during the Lawrence years. Perhaps *intensity* would describe my feelings more accurately, however. In the twenty-five years since the day I started my Yale education I had created a great many trials, tests and models of thought about education—trials, tests and models, I must say, that were to a large degree intuitive and even primitive. Out of this fusion of thought about education and practice in it came a sense that there were ways of using the mind and heart that in fact could liberate the individual from the burden of what Socrates called the unexamined life. This kind of educational experience was based not only in the *what* of the curriculum but in the *how* and *why* of it—the approach one took to what one read, calculated and experimented with. While the Rockefeller speech was a fair sample of my thinking at the time, my experience during the next forty-five years would give these convictions a trial and test that I could not even have imagined in the fall of 1963 when I left Lawrence. I would have to test these convictions on myself and through myself; I would be shaping patterns of life that it would take me years to understand.

In a simplified way, this test was already beginning. My sense of liberal learning was taking on a new shape; my emphasis on the humanities was valid but no longer adequate. The real issues of liberal learning lie beneath the humanities and reach beyond, into the enduring questions we ask of ourselves, questions that can be approached from many different disciplines of the mind. As we bring these questions to our active lives three simple words guide and challenge us. *What* is the problem? *Why* is it important? *How* do I deal with it most effectively? An honest response to these leads us into the complexity of the world and demands an equally complex response. In that response we use the best we have learned, and that *best* defines the nature of liberal learning. It is learning which leads to questions of value; what is better, what is worse?

I found that I was in a constant dialogue with myself. My first voice was searching, questioning, 'unfinished' in its thinking about complex problems; the second was urging me toward a decision, and constantly pushing the problem toward a new resolution, a more complex order. The dialogue is constantly present in effective administrative work, but in any field it shows itself through a willingness to resolve the complexities of a situation—to look into its heart rather than to come at it with an a priori mind-set. My mentor, Bill DeVane, said to me about the move to Lawrence, "Now you must learn to exercise infinite pity and infinite rigor." In other words, he was urging me to make use of my own liberal training. Above all I was to exercise both pity and rigor and not just contemplate or analyze them. I could not yet picture what a severe test this dialogue of complexity in action would receive in dealing with the stresses of the decade ahead, and how greatly it would help me to resolve many of the doctrinaire extremisms of the late 80s and 90s. It would guide me to decisions based on values (that abused word of the 90s) without the cookie-cutter definitions of them that would become so popular.

At the moment however, the Ford grant and a number of other fortunate successes within the college gave me a sense of optimism that was in direct parallel to the equally heady experience I was enjoying on the national scene. But I had no time to sit back in contemplation of my good fortune. In addition to our development of the college as a microcosm of the larger educational venture I worked at daily academic life and taught a variety of courses. This was an article of faith with me; undoubtedly I thought too well of myself at times during these years, but I never forgot the central meaning of the college. (I would do the same at Duke, in times when teaching seemed the only sane activity in my life.)

In 1961 there came to be another figure in the carpet, an emerging pattern woven into the ceaseless flow of college activity. As I have said, Lawrence had a unique reputation as the place which more than any other educated its Presidents and Deans for further work in the university world. This had been so striking in the case of my predecessor that I could not help but notice the increasing talk about my own future. In my fifth year at Lawrence I had been offered the Presidency of one of the best-known colleges in the country—and offered it over the telephone, and by trustees I had never met. I was still naive about such affairs, but I recognized arrogance when I heard it, and I declined that offer. Five years later I began to hear messages of a different sort.

Up to the 1960s the headhunters had not invaded the academic world; instead there was still the informal clearinghouse at the Carnegie Corporation. There one could hear about those who seemed most active and effective in their work as college presidents; from them the group of potential university presidents would emerge. It sounds wonderfully simple, but there was a great deal of informed thought behind the judgments made. Further, there was no attempt to cope in this way with the full array of institutional types and needs. Far too responsible to be regarded as an old boy network, this was a particular educational community in action. There were shared purposes among a certain group of institutions, and as a result there were shared qualifications for those who might head them.

In any case the 'community' had marked me as one of the two or three college presidents to be seriously considered for major university positions as they came along. Of course, for some time I did not know the inner workings of this system, which was much like the less codified but equally organized procedure that had brought me to Lawrence. What I did know was that inquiries began to appear in 1961. I had not indicated that I was available for this consideration, nor did I give the matter any heavy thought. There were some droll incidents—the best perhaps a call one evening while I was on summer vacation. Two senior administrators from Washington University announced that they were in the area and were quite insistent about seeing me. They were members of the Presidential Search Committee, cordial and quick with all the logical questions. I enjoyed the talk but was puzzled to hear only thunderous silence as the weeks went by. I mentioned this oddity to a highly knowledgeable friend, who broke into a broad grin and said, "Oh, you were on that list too, were you? Your two dinner partners had set up a neat routine; they interviewed a number of people, found them unsuitable for a variety of reasons and then gently put themselves forward for the two senior positions. Someone spotted the game, and the university had to start over with a new committee." Years later when I came to write this book I hesitated to tell this little story, but I decided that it was too revealing to leave in the closet. As my friend John Gardner, then President of Carnegie, remarked to me, "Yes, it's a fraud and a cheat; but, you know, what's worse is that sometimes they get away with it."

These skirmishes had no great meaning in themselves; they were simply warnings of a change in my personal weather. Suddenly, in the summer of 1962 things got very serious. Duke and Cornell turned up simultaneously, and both inquiries were heavy. This meant New York meetings with trustee committees ·from both places as well as inquiries on my part. Dean DeVane was uniquely fitted to comment; he was a South Carolinian who had taught at Cornell during a brief interlude in his Yale career. He favored Duke on the ground that Cornell was in fact several distinct parts of a university, and that it was difficult at times to develop a coherent plan of action. (And he felt further that this same difficulty carried over to the choosing of a president.) As matters developed, the Duke offer came first, and I accepted with a strong sense that there was something fated and inescapable about the choice. Little did I know how fated either choice would have been; I did have a strong intuitive sense, however, that the shift from Lawrence to Duke had dimensions other than size that would have to be confronted. This, as things turned out, was the understatement of a decade.

The experience of the years from 1946 to 1963 was intoxicating in pace and variety. Upon reflection I see the degree of luck involved in the events that took me so far so fast; I see the inevitable egotism that encouraged my acceptance of this frenetic life. And I see the possibility of conflict, the almost inevitable backlash against so much visibility and success. It is obvious to me now that such easy success can lead to frustration and suffering in a greatly changed setting and a radical shift in the attitudes of society. I knew how to handle myself in a situation of acceptance and success; I would learn how difficult the world of resistance and difficulty could be.

THE COMMODORE

I see the boats of summer at their moorings,
Riding against the wind, like great sea birds
Of such exotic shapes and plumage
It needs a book to classify them.

But books can't tell the love
That brought their tidy splendor into being.
Delight: There is no other word
For the dreams of men. Boys are not
In it, no matter how they try.
It takes an edge of conflict to explain
That varnish, those wonderful fittings, sails
So neatly furled. Don't deprive
Him of one afternoon. He needs them all
To counteract the poisons of his world.

CHAPTER FOUR:
The Duke Years

The Play and the Players
1963–1969

The 1960s are the pivotal point in this
story—equally so for the country and for me personally. In
1989 I wrote extensively about these years in *Street of Dreams,*
and my basic judgment about their many meanings has deepened in the ensuing years without changing in any central
way. I am more convinced than ever of their deep significance;
the temper of our society was permanently altered. Here I
concentrate on two matters: the public drama which emerged
in the course of the decade; and the personal drama of my
own academic career which was brought to an end in part by
the lethal power of the time.

There are several major concerns in that drama, and I can do
them justice only by separating them even though their power

came from the fact that they were not separable forces, but forces twisted together for greater strength.

For an understanding of the decade's energy and direction I turn to the start of the 60s, when Duke University and I committed ourselves to a highly active program with national implications. The everyday life of the university is seen and embodied in the work of the President, which moves dramatically during the decade to another kind of effort as major crisis-driven events penetrate and reshape the life of the institution—and equally of its President. In the special case of Duke this complexity did not stand alone.It was complicated by the Board of Trustees and also by a major source of financial support, the Duke Endowment, which had its own sense of power and definition of educational purpose.

The dance at this point becomes a ballet of conflict, and the dancer discovers dimensions of his own life that had been concealed, not only from his previous knowledge but also from his whole prior experience of the university world. My personal trauma and that of my society will echo and mirror each other; I end the decade as an exile, while the society ends it in disunity and violence at many levels. For a brief time melodrama becomes the norm, while the sanity of normal life seems a dream, utopian and unattainable.

I indicated in the Lawrence chapter that I had picked up by 1960 some hint of a coming change in the attitudes of young people. There it was simply a sense that the ocean was in motion, telegraphing that some dramatic shift in attitude was on the way. For me it was also the reading on a seismograph, and the very intensity of the public response to the Camelot myth should have told us how ready one whole segment of society was for a change of language, a new idiom by which to speak and think about itself. That was one major reason for the reaction to the President's murder; it was the murder of a future just beginning to be felt, a dream that was most alluring because it was so totally untested.

This shock was uniquely destabilizing for the generation just coming to college, because its members were too young to rejoice (as their immediate elders could) in the peace and hope that underlay the upbeat life of the 1950s. They felt the urgencies of the cold war, for example, without any of the stabilizing personal commitments already made to love and career. They became both the center of the storm to come and the measure of it. When their activist elders took up several major causes, it was university students who provided the followers—and some leaders—as well as the chief arena for action, on the campuses of the major universities.

The universities themselves were the perfect places to intensify every conflict. They were taken to be hotbeds of free thinkers and "pinko liberals" in the idiom of Board members and older alumni whose devotion to alma mater consisted often in a determined effort to maintain it as they *imagined* it had been when they were undergraduates. Above all, they wanted no 'radical' attitudes to spoil that dream, since for the most part they had little patience with the four concerns that came together to create the remarkable texture of conflict during the decade.

The first concern was native to the undergraduate world itself: the alienation of students, with their inevitable cry for 'relevance'—a trend that I had noted in the later 1950s, when I found it astringent and stimulating and very much to the point in defining the living center of good educational encounter. What I did not recognize was its prehensile quality. As other major issues began to command heavy support they flowed onto the campuses and became absorbed in the general ferment that included suddenly aggressive black and women's movements, as well as the dark vortex of Vietnam. As this became a steadily more disturbing issue it assumed the role of catalyst, the perfect ground and rallying cry for the other concerns. In *Street of Dreams* I described the result of all of this as a kind of Buckminster Fuller construction, where each major element can no longer be isolated from the whole, and each lends intensity and stability to the other. It was inevitable that the conservative elders would be both outraged and defensive at the tremendous energy that these four movements generated—and above all when they began to reinforce each other in speech and action. Those activist elders who were so vocally devoted to one or the other of these massive issues could not by themselves have generated a tenth of the explosive power created when university students put the whole chemistry together.

If this tangle of causes was a concern for the country as a whole and the universities in particular, it was designed to cause unique trouble for a privileged, private and in many ways conservative Southern university. I was aware of these potential difficulties, but in the fall of 1963 they were still latent. Certainly I was not fully aware of the silent discomfort that my own antecedents were causing to many of my new friends. As my mother (who had both lived in North Carolina as a girl and taught there later) pointed out, "When I saw the Durham paper's headline, *Yankee Born and Yale Educated,* I knew you were in for trouble." It is only fair to say, however, that even with this liability I could have managed if each of the main issues of the 60s had not cut directly across so many of the convictions and traditions of the university and the region. I had trouble understanding the multiple dynamics of the period, but many of those around me had no trouble at all; they were outraged by what they saw as the impudence and lack of respect in undergraduates, the displaced standards of the women's movement, the assertiveness of blacks who were in the university only on sufferance, and the anti-Vietnam stance of the whole student population which ran directly counter to the chivalric-military traditions of the South.

The coalescence of these major concerns was not, of course, evident while it was being shaped. The separate movements had first to become viable individually; then they found each other. At times the discovery was the revelation of a long-standing relationship that had long been submerged; the coalescence of the black and women's movements for instance was driven by a recognition of common bondage, which had been articulated before the civil war by numbers of bold and independent women. Under the impact of so deep a *malaise,* the connection was revived. Similarly, the southern chivalric and military tradition was also locked into a relationship with the violent anti-war agitation; it was an inverse relation, of course, but an extremely powerful one. Eighty percent of the general officers in all three services had come from the South; their professional loyalty was guided all too easily into a judgment that opposition to the war came very close to treason. At the same time their honest patriotism was painted by their young opponents as the backward and bloodthirsty attitude of professional butchers. The rallying cry of 'relevance' in education then became a supporting substructure for these other issues, so that the intensity of emotion generated was squared and cubed by their intimate interaction.

And once again history played catalyst in several critical ways. The three assassinations were major destabilizing events, and the war itself became a constant destructive force—its own worst enemy. Every major claim of victory seemed to have its counterpart in photographs of frightened children and devastated land. Pretences about the war were being unmasked as rapidly as they were advanced, so that the image of a very bad war became dominant. Almost as a reciprocal of this devastating and years-long event, President Johnson's genuine effort for massive social reform was destroyed. The money that would have sustained it went to Vietnam, and the President was effectively neutralized along with his dream. The distrust of government then became a fifth element in the turbulence through which the universities (beyond all other institutions) had to grope their way.

As a final irony of the decade, the universities, which offered so perfect a setting for disruption, were also the most vulnerable to disruption. They are, after all, places of civility and debate rather than insult and confrontation. Whenever irrational strife takes over the community suffers; the vision of the university is for that time diminished and Dante's *vita diritta* is lost. The late sixties were one of those times of great loss, with consequences still alive nearly forty years later. I witnessed the changes as they unfolded, and I was deeply involved in a good many. I could certainly never claim that I saw and understood fully what others and I were doing to hold our places together. I can only unfold the daily patterns of life and the crises that made up the texture of that time for me.

The months between my November 1962 election and our arrival in Durham the following August were themselves singular. I decided that it would be unfair to leave Lawrence until a successor was found. This was not just ego talking; a small place loses its inertial drive easily. Everything at Lawrence was moving well, and I did not want to spoil it. As a result I decided to commute to Duke every other weekend; the routine simply devoured energy, of course, but I was forty-one and believed I had everything and to spare. I learned much about Duke even though I missed a great deal of the power politics that would plague me later. The worst of it was screened from me, but I knew enough to get a few extremely helpful answers to my questions.

I knew that I was walking into a deeply divided university community; with all the arrogance of a successful ten years behind me I felt certain that I could deal with it, that there must be a perfectly logical answer though the contending groups were simply too blinded by conflict to see clearly. In fact, I would find the issues so savage that I would have to describe them and face them in detail a few years later. Further, the truth would in fact show so dark and unswerving an animosity that I would not see the depth of it fully for another thirty-five years. Now I would settle for the belief that tranquility—at least official tranquility—had been reestablished. One of the senior members of the medical faculty accepted the chore of interim president for three years and gave the university public time enough to quiet down. With that pious hope of stability, and on the best assurances I could get from everyone, I stepped into the uneasy quiet of one of the most beautiful campuses in America.

More accurately, we all stepped in by station wagon late one August morning, to find an official house crammed with our boxes and furniture. Two deeply apprehensive maids were waiting for these outsiders, these strange Yankees. (They and their daughters would become our truly helpful assistants and friends.)

But what of the university? Like Lawrence, it was poised on the edge of a tumultuous decade. As I pointed out in *Street of Dreams*, at the start of the 1960s Duke was a university under stress and also in inevitable transition. The stress related above all to tension between the Duke Endowment board of trustees and some senior administrators on the one hand, and certain members of the university administration and Board on the other. After the resignation of President Hollis Edens and vice president Paul Gross the question of final responsibility for the university's welfare would remain unresolved for a decade.

I was joining a university with great potential stature and a major role to play both nationally and in its own quadrant of the country. It was *not* equipped, by nature and location, to absorb sudden change of any kind, let alone disruptive challenges. Its admission of the first black undergraduates had not yet been digested, nor had the complexity of doing justice to their needs been faced. I have just spoken of attitudes and problems internal to Duke; this question of black education was national, as would be the kindred issues of the war, the position of women in our society, and the great question of the concept of the university itself. All of this was already present, hovering over the university world that would be the perfect locus for the passionate interaction of these causes. All that was needed was the catalyst; it came with the murder of John Kennedy on November 22, 1963. I was just settling in with a group of senior administrators who showed the real quality of the university in their eagerness to work with me for the good of the whole place. We would, with few exceptions, develop a great loyalty to one another. The assassination put this to the immediate test in a macabre way. *The Game* between Carolina and Duke was to be played in a few days and one of my first rational thoughts was that it would be an obscene thing to do. I called the Executive Secretary of the NCAA, who replied piously that "we are recommending a moment of respectful silence." I was under high stress, but my own clarity surprised me. "You can recommend what you damned please, but Duke isn't going to play a game this Saturday." The repercussions were lively; it turned out, of course, that many of my constituents had no love for JFK and managed to ignore the true meaning of the murder. As the Director of Athletics said to me, "Well, you're the boss; go ahead, and I'll head for the hills."

That 'true meaning' would be asserting itself in the country for the rest of the decade and well beyond. I doubted in the first days that we could go ahead with the plans for university development, which I already had in place. It turned out that we could, but everything had changed in subtle ways, as though a filter had been put over a lens, and the whole landscape of the country had been shifted, had turned gray. Plans and actions had a sense of partiality or subtle injury about them; many years later I would remember this diminishing of life, which at the same time drew to itself concerns that were already becoming critical. This was a first fracturing of a state of civility, which was still quite evident at the start of the sixties. The conflicts of the decade were so contentious, and they cut so deep into individual lives, that a whole new vocabulary emerged—violent, often obscene and tending to pose each issue in its confrontational form. Costume, hair, beards came to supplement language in creating a total atmosphere which had an astonishing effect on the elders. I found it hard twenty or thirty years later to believe that the irritations of the young had succeeded so well. Certainly this was the only time in my life where I was pressured to censor costumes as well as publications. I could endure the four-letter attacks in the student newspaper; I simply stopped reading it. I found it extremely abrasive to endure the constant carping of the elders, however, which in time became as mindless as the jargon of the young.

Civility may have been one chief casualty of the 60s. (The aggressive style of the 90s had, I later thought, its origin in these intemperate years. The verbalism of the university world was all too easily shaped into a new rhetoric whose ugliness was made a substitute for any genuine vigor of thought.) There was an equal casualty in the loss of balance in the daily lives of the young, who were caught up most forcefully in the major movements. Everything seemed heightened almost to frenzy by external troubles, and then the frenzy became a cause in itself. I realized with one corner of my mind that this development was a predictable one for any mass movement so driven by emotion (and weren't they all?). But I was too heavily involved in the day's work to give this detached analysis the attention it later received in *Street of Dreams.*

All that went on in the 60s to give it that unique quality of interlocked destruction and creation was for the most part a context for my daily life rather than the center. It intervened violently at times—as in the 'visit' at the house and the occupation of Allen Administration Building—but there was usually a tandem experience which shaped my working life. Obviously the 'outer' world could not be ignored; its pressure was almost constant. But the normal and many-sided job of the presidency was the absorbing center, and I used it as far as possible to push back the 'alien' demands and distortions. I had developed by the end of my Lawrence years a clear sense of duties and priorities; now I put them into play, as I discovered that—as Nathan Pusey said to me about the similarity between Lawrence and Harvard—the addition of a few zeroes in the financial statement had little to do with the essential jobs. Both places needed what I was within limits able to do; they had significant reputations which were not in fact borne out by their reality. Lawrence was financially *very* limited, while Duke was complacent, too willing to rely on the Endowment for its financial needs. I thought so and said so in many speeches, starting with the first just a month after my election and eight months before I arrived on campus. (If I had understood the depth of the Endowment Trustees' desire for control, I would have seen how quickly I complicated my relation to them.)

My zeal to broaden the base of support had a force driving it which was outside my perception of the problems to be solved. I had just finished a Ford grant for Lawrence, and was receiving intimations that the same might be done for Duke. This would involve not only money, but the long-range planning which the university so badly needed, if for no other reason than to stabilize it after the recent traumas. If I could get some consensus on a development plan, I would have coherence in my uses of myself. As this plan developed at Duke, it became clear that the size of the grant would be limited by a past lack of sustained fund raising effort, while the high matching ratio—three to one—was a clear signal of what the potential ability of the university was. Obviously I was pleased to be the only recipient of a Ford grant for two different institutions, but I did not anticipate how much the troubles of the 60s would interfere with our efforts.

I brought to bear on the project all the technical development skills I had learned, and I had some able outside help. My major job, however, continued to be an extension of the purpose I outlined in that first major speech: to establish the national position of the university without disrupting its strong regional obligations and strengths. (My best evidence that I had succeeded came to me years later in public testimony from my successor—the former governor of the state—and from the current governor. Both acknowledged that I had started the new direction, the new concept of the university's scope. That reality was by no means clear to me in the conflicts at the end of the 60s.)

How was it done and, specifically, what was accomplished beyond the large redirection of the university—in short, to give substance to those grand words? A good deal that would qualify for edifice building, new educational programs and a firming-up of direction embodied in one major shift of the physical plant. In six years the major commitments were made for a doubled library, new biomedical research space and clinical facilities were added; dormitory space was augmented—together with many customary essential matters.

Of new problems in the use of space the most important was the successful effort on my part to take a nearly useless science building on the east campus and turn it into an Art Museum which would become one of the most dynamic parts of the university. An equally vigorous future was in store for the embryo School of Business, which a gifted young economist and I agreed to start on one bright day in the mid-sixties. The Art Museum was fought through against some heavy Philistine ridicule; the Business School flowed like hot butter.

A major physical shift, one with implications very dear to my heart, resulted from the necessity to find adequate low cost housing in Durham. Some simple apartments were available for purchase, and they happened to be directly across the road from our graduate student apartment complex. Trustee agitation: "We must buy the apartments to keep low-income tenants out of our area." I: "Why not sell HUD *our* property instead; then we can build in the area between the two ends of our campus—an area not yet developed?" Agreed and done. When the horrid realization came that for the first time there would be black residents in the western part of Durham, I refused to change the plan. Two main goals were met at once: adequate public housing for the city and the beginning of a unified campus—the latter accomplished against the wishes of certain faculty and administrators who wanted to perpetuate a separate woman's college in the fine Trinity

College buildings at the eastern end of the total campus area.

The importance of this summary lies in the fact that a tumultuous decade did not block the normal progress of our university development. There was abnormal effort required to achieve these 'normal' results, and they were for a time obscured by all the tumult, but they survived without much damage or even hindrance.

In fact, I came to feel that I had done as much as the years allowed me in my effort to turn Duke toward its full status as a national university. And certainly my wife and I together put as much effort into the President's job as anyone could have managed. Though we did not know it, we were among the last to conceive of that responsibility in the old dual pattern, which made us the official host and hostess of the university. We had been told to replace the original President's house, which stood at the main entrance to the west campus, and we designed the new one to help us with our job. We went to see Alden Dow, one of the most imaginative of Frank Lloyd Wright's pupils (we had seen some striking examples of his work); together we laid out the chief purposes of the place and developed what we would call University House in a vain effort to indicate that it was not in any way our private residence. We failed at this, in part because the boldness of the building came to be identified with our own style, and in part because the community did not grasp the basic concept that we believed necessary. There we entertained about ten thousand guests a year, from official university visitors who stayed with us to visiting musical groups (which often gave informal concerts in the House) to the many campus groups that needed the cachet of a central university setting. In this part of our work we succeeded well; the fact was proven by our successor, who did not want the burden of living in the house but renamed it the President's Guest House, where it served all the functions we established for it. For us, of course, it became a defining part of our lives, and in the worst of the late sixties my office there became my only quiet workspace.

There were, of course, all of the external commitments to national committees and enterprises; these assumed a special pressure and demand since they had to be carried on in the face of the daily crises. As with the progress we made within the university, the external work was by and large effective—and in the case of the National Commission on Libraries quite surprisingly so. I was asked by the White House to chair this venture; we carried on our interviewing and other deliberations at the worst time (during 1968) and amazingly our report survived the change of administrations to become a permanent organization. (And I am told that the report we produced has become a benchmark in library stud-·ies.)

The teaching which I did during these years must not be seen as one more burden; it was my refuge and my delight, and I told my students that they were the sane oases in an absurd world. But the teaching, and the poetry, which asserted itself during these years, could not resolve one intimate and profound problem. That aspect of this wild time I had to keep totally within myself— the certain knowledge that every day in the later sixties I was burning more energy—more of myself—than I could replenish. I could not live on the interest; instead I was using up the capital of my mind and body, with no reasonable hope of protecting and restoring either one. Life had become relentless, and I could do nothing to change it. This may sound melodramatic; certainly it seems so to me in retrospect, while I was totally clear that the melodrama was real, and that it seemed to occur in some new form every day.

One consequence was a serious derangement of my normal schedule. I came to dread the mornings, which had always been my best working time, because disruption seemed to come with the daylight. My only peaceful working hours came at night— usually about 1:00 to 3:00—when I could cover a great deal of correspondence and handle the preparation for the endless committee meetings which the difficult time demanded. At that hour, too, I was free from the telephone—the greatest blessing of all. Years later I could look back at these stratagems and smile a bit, but at the time they were a necessity.

Perhaps the flavor of the days could best be caught by the 4:15 calls from the Chairman of the Board, (also the vice president and General Counsel of the Ford Motor Company). He worked for a driving boss, and (as his wife told me) he drove others in turn. After he finished his daily struggles to satisfy Henry Ford II he would pick out some vexing subject, start the attack with, "I understand that the matter is still hanging fire," and away we would go. Sometimes there was no real issue, sometimes the problem was insoluble, but the phone call could be counted on. There was the same heavy burden about it that I found, near the start of my time at Duke, when a noisily pious trustee discovered that the chief proponent of the "God is Dead" theological fad was to speak at the Duke Divinity School. This trustee would not, could not, dared not accept the fact that the national Methodist organization had arranged the visit and paid for the lecture. After a dozen letters another Trustee called me aside at a meeting and said, "Just give it up, Doug; you'll never get through to him." As the tensions of the time mounted, these contretemps took on both might and edge. All the old jokes—being nibbled to death by ducks, and the like—became an awful reality.

These were normal aspects of Trustee-President relationships, and they would not have loomed large if the times had not been so far from normal. In addition to the Duke Endowment with its own agenda (which will be discussed separately) there were the profound cultural shocks of the time. Black undergraduates were new at Duke, and a strong minority of the Trustees had been opposed to their admission. The same, alas, turned out to be true of the alumni during these troubles; each critical event compounded those before it, and I found myself riding a historic wave, which—according to my constituents— I should have been able to control. As the Chairman said, "I don't care what's happening in the country, I don't want it here."

The particular sequence of events which became my long moment of crisis included the murder of Martin Luther King, Jr. with its aftermath in our house, the students' silent vigil for better staff working conditions which followed, and the incendiary visit of Dick Gregory the following winter, which produced the occupation of the central administrative offices by *all* of the sixty-seven black students at Duke. The motivations of the students, white and black, were thoroughly understandable, quite honorable, and in the case of the vigil highly effective. For me the result was a high wire balancing act—on one side the legitimate urgen-

cies of the time, and on the other a passionate effort to keep the
essential activities of the university moving ahead. The result was
quite predictable; sooner or later I would jump or I would be
pushed.

The end of the decade was marked by a remarkable coalescence of forces; the major issues which created the national social
upheaval were paralleled at Duke by a coalescence of groups
which in twenty years would seem to everyone involved a bad
dream, something which of course could not have happened. At
the moment, there was substantial agreement among Trustees,
the Duke Endowment, the regional community, and a disturbing
number of alumni, that the situation was out of control and that
I had failed to control it. I protected the black students against
enormous—almost gleeful—pressure to dismiss them; but like
the bee with one sting I could not protect myself.

Duke had one unique element of its structure, which was to
give me serious trouble, as it had for my predecessors. James B.
Duke decided in the early 1920s to create a major university on
the base given by Trinity College, (which his father had moved to
Durham from the country many years before). James B. Duke
had also other plans to help the two Carolinas, and he created the
Duke Endowment in 1924 as a Foundation devoted to undergraduate colleges, medical care and rural church life as well as to
Duke University. There were certain conditions over which the
Endowment trustees had a watchdog function—fiscal stability
chief among them. In addition, there were crossover memberships established on the Endowment Board, the University Board
and the Duke Power Company.

As J. B. Duke saw it the triple relationship would benefit
everyone. Common sense would suggest many dangers in this
structure, however. The Duke Endowment Board was made up
of members of James B. Duke's close circle and their successors;
money rather than education was their primary concern, but they
arranged in various ways to maintain their control over the separately elected University Board of Trustees. This extremely
muddy situation had led to serious interference with educational
policy in the 1930s and an all-out brawl in the late 1950s involving both Boards, the University President and an ambitious vice

president. The ambitious vice president was by 1962 educational advisor to the Duke Endowment and still active on campus.

My informants—in particular the interim President—reassured me but without unfolding the full ugliness of the struggle. My first personal encounter (I did not yet know that the Endowment group were cool to my appointment) came in a little private list of people whom (I was told) it would be wise to remove from their jobs. These included the highly respected Provost, the executive secretary to the President, the business manager and several others of importance. I checked a bit, recognized a vendetta, and threw the list away. I was right, of course; without these people I would have had to accept the Endowment's choices, and they would have established their control over me and the university in a highly restrictive way. They would not forget, however, and they became vindictive in the extreme. Of the forces to be reckoned with, this was potentially the most destructive—or would have been in normal times. I would have to deal with them constantly and would understand the full situation only thirty years later.

And with the glorious irony which history gives us once in a while, I would learn this full truth about my purgatory experience from a history of the Endowment written with total access to all the records by the Duke University historian, Robert Durden— an inconceivable event in my time. There I discovered that a former Duke faculty member now employed by the Endowment as an educational consultant, was determined not only to bring about the dismissal of the distinguished Provost, but to control me as well. He had ambitions of his own to represent educational policy for all of the Endowment institutions. As a result we had many points of intersection and—alas—conflict.

Failing in his efforts at direct control he became a town crier of petty alarms and foolish excursions. As Durden points out, any of the normal frictions of an active university were presented to the Endowment as failures of administrative leadership. Each summer storm emerged as a typhoon, and the Endowment Board was encouraged to believe what it feared most—some 'failure of fiscal responsibility.' This became the major route of attack on me, and it combined beautifully with the turbulence of the late sixties.

The figures of our financial progress (190 million of support in six years, triple that of the preceding period) should have refuted these criticisms; instead they were turned into nervous nelly doubts; the percentage of Endowment support dropped, and this fact was taken to be a sign that the university was unstable—about as false an interpretation of the facts as one could possibly manage.

All of this was carried on behind my back; I never had an honest chance to deal with it, and the Endowment Chairman was able to create a sense of fear among the university trustees, which was then combined with constant veiled threats of the withdrawal of Endowment support. As I look back I am amazed that I was able to hold my place and encourage as much growth in six years as actually took place.

This action played itself out in ways that were for the most part clandestine, but they were sustained in ways that reached into many parts of the university. The Endowment had to be cautious; the recent tangle had been too obvious and heavy-handed. Now they would seek to exert control by bribery and assert that control by exploiting the turbulence of the time. Their animosity was ironic in the extreme, for I was leading the university toward its national goals and purposes—exactly what they had said they wanted. Their passion for control, however, obscured everything else. Large block grants were offered as a bribe to my Medical Center friends, who rejected them angrily. Then a market downturn caused an operating deficit—temporary but disturbing—and I was accused of fiscal imprudence—even though MIT (on whose governing Board I was serving at the time) and Harvard were having the same experience. Finally the aggressive behavior of our black students created the political opening my Endowment critics had waited for. There was such protest from the alumni and the regional community over their occupation of the administrative offices that I could be accused of losing control. I lost the battle, but I won the war of independence for the university. The Endowment finally put itself on the road of responsibility rather than manipulative control, and it became the great private foundation it is today.

INNER AND OUTER LIVES: The Sixties Within

I realized as I looked back at those years that two major concerns in my life had little to do with my stated responsibility as President of the University. My teaching and my poetry were far more than the preoccupations which replaced golf or sailing as the defining actions of my leisure. They were in fact my attempts to move in a world both more intimate and more profound than anything the university presidency could offer. They kept the often horrible daily life of the late 1960s at bay; when I told my classes that it was their job to keep me sane, I was not far from the literal truth; certainly my daily tasks were often exercises in the insane and the irrelevant.

The poetry was perhaps the most curious and revealing aspect of life at this time—curious because on the face of it a time when I was preoccupied with a thousand matters should have left no room for Wordsworth's emotion recollected in tranquility. In any case, my experience was totally different from any expectation I could have imagined. One night during our second fall at Duke I was "disposing myself to sleep" when suddenly there was a voice, cool and neutral—not the line of a poem, I later realized, but a voice. "Get up; I have a poem for you." "Go away, go away," was my reaction. I had written verse as a young man, but critical appraisal had kept me from showing it to anyone else. "No, no; I mean it," said the voice. "Get up." So I did, and forty-five minutes later I found this, lying on the desk in front of me. It was not automatic writing, but it was *commanded* to me then, demanded from me.

NEGRO FARM: JANUARY

What hope of spring lies in this earth,
Littered with last year's corn, raped
Casually by a plough, an uncertain mule?
What seedy chariot carries to town
The two-bit dreams of its tenants, rained on
Like gravestones, by the impersonal storms of winter?

What damp Ezekiel sits by the red road
Watching the wheels, and dreaming of what Heaven?
His eye catches the clay bank, blurs into mud,
I think, but I know nothing
Of the whorled fern he can conjure up
In its dirt bed, the sleeping dogwood in his rubble,
Or the sleep in his brute house, which could be love.

I cannot share it, shut out
By all the unplanned arrogance of my place,
A costly Assyrian, whisked off to the city,
Moving in bright blindness, to seek out
Through habit the savage distractions of my palace.

It was the first of a group, which over the next six years would become *The Dark Gate*, an extended collection of verse—extended, because the poems showed up with great regularity. I never again needed the prompting which was prelude to that first one, but that commanding moment lent great authenticity and confidence to everything that came after it.

Those who have not had such an encounter may smile at my total reliance on the voice, thinking it some simple trick of the mind with no 'objective' existence. Most artists understand; certainly I knew—indeed I more than knew: I *was*, quite simply, in the presence of something other than myself. It was an encounter reaching into what we naively set aside as the primitive experience of man's understanding. Certainly it goes back as far as we humans go; it is a type of creative encounter with an external reality, which can be neither explained nor explained away. I had no doubt of the significance of the event; it was as though the cork came out of the bottle—the result just as homely and unaffected as any other natural and relevant event. That was a major aspect of the power that the poems had over me. They were important because they had this direct authenticity in a world that had in many ways lost it. One of the great paradoxes of the sixties lies in the collapse of well-grounded perception both in the passionate young and in their stiff-necked elders. They were increasingly in the grip of a *position,* that fatal enemy of responsible thought; to this my poetry was a major antidote, though none of those around me could have seen it for what it was. In fact, they did not see it at all.

My teaching was precious to me for exactly the same reason; I did not articulate its full reality at the time, though I felt its presence and its importance constantly. There was, in fact, a dimension to the material I taught which made it a remarkable corrective to the destructive nonsense I lived with every day. My special teaching interest, the European epic tradition, had an inescapable ethical dimension. A generation later some so-called scholars would try to dissolve this dimension of meaning in the acid of their critical bias; for me, however, these great works of literature were talismans, warding off the evils of trivial thought and ego-centered action. They explored good and evil without easy moralism and they created a depth of judgment, a mythic strength for me when it was absolutely essential. Among the voices of discord they were voices of judgment and insight. At the same time, they were intensely private; those around me saw only their impact on my actions.

But neither the poetry nor the teaching could save me, of course, when history closed in. Nor could I escape a larger and longer-lasting version of historical pressure by attempting to go back to the books and the poetry in a return to full-time teaching. I was clear about this, and found it ironic beyond imagining, that these very sources of strength which saw me through the worst times must still be subordinated to some other pattern—

and a pattern which I must create for myself. I must step out of the university world, with all the sustaining strength of its great traditions; it had been my life, and now I could not tolerate it. What should I do? My curious fate, which brought me to this point, had a place ready for my future, but the path to it would lead through some dark places. That path would also be shaped by perceptions and limits equally alive in me and in the historic setting I inhabited.

Though I had no time or energy to ponder it, I was living out a major encounter with that setting. My career had been exceptionally swift; if the pace of my advancement had been conventional I would not have been in this place at this moment. My success, in short, guaranteed my defeat. When I could see clearly, I realized that I was a tiny example of that doom the Greeks knew so well. *Moira* was the inescapable fate; one could do something beyond it if he survived, but he could not alter it. "My friends, we cannot escape history." Lincoln in the 1860s was dealing with the same reality, but in its most extreme form. The nineteen-sixties would in a lesser way leave a major scar across the pattern and culture of the country, and I would have the dark privilege of bearing the same scar across my personal life.

That sentence may seem to have a "Sorrows of Young Werther" quality; it needs a bit of explanation. The times became so extreme in the late 60s that the rhetoric for describing them was equally so. And it was a rhetoric of action as well as phrase. After the Allen Building occupation and the savage reaction of the regional community we had a guard at the house every night. We also sent our youngest son to stay with friends every evening— "I don't like this going away from home," was his heart-breaking statement—and I found myself wandering around the perimeter of the house at night with a loaded pistol in my dressing gown pocket. Ridiculous, yes; foolish, no. These actions were vital aspects of my life and the life of the region.

But there were far deeper issues. Part of my internal/external disruption at the end of the sixties was my difficulty in facing and appraising myself properly. I had treated my Lawrence and Duke relationships in a highly committed and totally personal way. I never made a material demand. I never planned a strategy for protecting myself in the face of opposition. In fact, I ignored the political issues once I had made up my mind about the best course of action for myself as the servant of the place. That was how I saw myself, as the servant. I was given the opportunity to think and act in this quixotic and emotionally involved way; I continued to accept it through the increasingly tangled events of the late 1960s.

I have indicated that my earlier successes, and the fact that I had started the president's job so early in my career, contributed to make me highly vulnerable now. I had had none of that sobering experience in a career which comes from hopes not fulfilled, pathways blocked. A whole range of experience which might have given me some distance and perspective in appraising my situation was simply not available. I had not thought about other career paths, while in any case the intensity of my state of mind kept some logical ones from any serious consideration. I sensed that I could not consider another university position, so that a faculty appointment elsewhere was not feasible. (In fact, I found the trauma so deep that for several years I could not spend time on a university campus at all—even for the graduation of our third son.) As a result, I did not evolve a plan, any more than with the Lawrence and Duke appointments; I let the plan come to me.

I had to live with the reality, however; there was a fracture of my lifetime commitment to my academic career. As I look back thirty years later, with a whole new pattern of life firmly in place, I can see how perilous and yet how filled with promise this moment was. I must reckon in some new way with my talents, but even more deeply with my need for inner balance in the face of this exile, this total break with my past. As I have said, I took comfort from Aeneas and his need to find that new world, and I would discover that I shared with all other exiles the false paths, the self-doubts, and ultimately the surprise of finding that the destination—the one which would ultimately establish a remarkable but eccentric continuity with my past—was different from anything I could possibly have imagined or planned for myself. The journey of defeat would turn into a voyage of discovery.

In a curious way this would also be true of the whole country. The fracture line in our national self-image came exactly here, and the guilt, which expressed itself so wretchedly in our first reaction to the Vietnam veterans was a major sign of it. The 70s would be a sleazy decade in many ways, but one of the chief would be in our reluctance to face up to the wrong we had done, not only to the Vietnamese but to ourselves in that misguided and brutal war. In my tiny way I was setting forth, like the country at large, to find myself again in new settings and by mastering a different way of life.

I was setting out after the loss of my innocence, exactly as the country would; and I was no more ready than the country to call it that. For the country at large this took the form of a denial that the war expressed a profound moral commitment, but that the commitment was wrong, and that in fact the final result was morality stood on its head. Step by step we got into that war as an anti-communist crusade. We ignored the warnings of the French, and we created the ugliest possible spectacle of ourselves *to* ourselves. Our own soldiers became scapegoats before we finally returned to our senses.

In my case (to compare small things with great) the denial took the form of a multi-year pretense that I had moved logically and easily from university to corporate world, that I was comfortable and coherent in my new work, and that I was 'doing the right thing.' The first five years of the 70s decade would show how wrong I was. The mask I wore in those years concealed me further from myself and from the full meaning of my experience at the time.

For amid these cascading images there were glimpses of the great enduring structures of the decade described in the opening section of this chapter. I could not hold them firmly in mind, however, and I realized later that there was a curious reason for my inability (quite apart from the sheer fatigue of those days). My whole training and experience to this point had been based in a concept of the university and of liberal education totally grounded in mediation, critical discourse, civility and the restraint of uncontrolled dogmatism. Now I found that I was required to set all this aside, and to respond instead to issues which were not for me the most enduring ones. As a result I spent—and overspent—my energy where I did not want to put it, and so the action of the late 60s was for me a divided action. I was pulled between what I knew the university needed over the decades and what the times demanded immediately. It was a schizophrenia with only one inevitable outcome, and I would reflect on its meaning for years, always in the recognition that my whole career had put me in a place and point of time from which there was no honorable escape.

The trauma and fault line for the country were dramatic. My reflection on the 60s led me even at that time to a cluster of judgments about the period which suggest something of its power and diversity. Some were well-known and became steadily more so with time: the loss of innocence over the Vietnam War, the sexual revolution that came with new contraceptive means, the sense of rebellion and the quest for relevance. All these are too familiar, perhaps; they obscure other and more enduring changes of attitude and insight.

The range of these is remarkable: the impetus toward religious diversity, an equal movement toward singularities of style in clothing and modes of life, ethical assertiveness and aggressiveness, the rediscovery of the skills of hand and eye that make for fine craftsmanship, a sense that education is both a communal and individual matter. These patterns will, after some hiatus in the 1970s, become steadily more significant in American culture. They will also represent my private experience writ very large indeed, both in the grave short-term trauma and in the enduring change.

These concerns were equally vital and demanding for me and my culture. One proof of that fact lies in the drabness and shallow conformity of the 1970s, where the very conformities demonstrate the degree of turmoil created by the sixties. It had been overwhelming, and society seemed to draw back from it. But the changed life-styles proved far stronger than their critics in the 1970s believed. Many of the far-out positions of the 60s became viable alternate life-styles and would be a major influence on the eclectic and multiple value systems of the 90s. Above all, perhaps, the 60s contributed heavily to a questioning, restless and dissatisfied style of life which would assert itself in conflicts as diverse as the abortion issue, the use of drugs at various levels of destructiveness, and the redefinition of family and social structures to accommodate a whole cluster of new economic and ethical realities. The great continuity would establish itself; in time the 60s would come to be a decade, not of neglected excesses and extremes of behavior but of initiations and new directions. And so of course it proved for me; I found under duress a new way of life, which would prove to be richly nurtured by my past.

THE LIGHT

Light enters; the clear glass of mind
Accepts, focuses, makes shapes
Where a great whiteness was.
The wonderful might-be becomes
A tangible Eve, a rock,
A serpent in his beauty, dazzling
Innocence, turning to fire
The promise of morning, evening's kiss
And the incredible, starry night
That shaped love's lullabies.
All perfect things descend to clay,
Those first incredible moments burned away
To harsh words, images, regrets,
Yet with some echo of bright memory.

CHAPTER FIVE:
The Dark Journey
1969-1976

It is the height of impudence to mention

Aeneas and myself in the same sentence—but there are two useful similarities. Each individual (Aeneas becomes a mythic figure in the course of the Aeneid) was hurting intensely; and each was unaware of the real meaning of the ordeal he was to undergo. It would take me longer than Aeneas, in fact, to understand where and who I now was. (Aeneas had some formidable inducement, after all; he was allowed to see the gods fork down the walls of Troy, as Virgil puts it.) I had to intuit my situation, and for some years I was almost totally unsuccessful at this.

My new encounters differed from any that had preceded them, though they shared an unexpectedness and excitement that often brought out a highly favorable—and uncritical—response in me. A letter from the RCA vice president for education (who was retiring) asked if I might be interested in the job. I knew that I could not go to another university. I refused to admit what this extreme fatigue—almost nausea—had to tell me, but the fact itself was overwhelming. The thought of a totally different setting brought life back, and I accepted the RCA job. I stepped out of a world which had supported and given structure to my life for thirty-one years; now I must discover—if I could—how to make sense of a new and, it seemed, quite alien world. (I would not know until some years later that the world I stepped into was having the same problems of identity, effectiveness, engagement as I.)

The surfaces of my new job were glittering enough; the mandate of the RCA vice president for education was fuzzy (and became steadily more so) but the outer trappings included not only the New York office but a staff group near the old RCA establishment in Camden, and Directorships in several RCA subsidiaries. These gave me a window on that curious moment in the history of major American corporations when acquisition became a passion almost as unthinking as the Dutch Tulip craze or the Florida boom. For a few years acquisition was a given, an automatic good; incredibly enough, Random House was acquired to bolster the education enterprise (so that I became a Director) while Hertz Cars (again I was involved) was RCA's link to the world of transportation. Most irrational and expensive of all was a move into the mainframe computer industry.

As a footnote to this expensive failure, I would meet an IBM vice president in Iran a few years later. When I referred to the computer debacle my counterpart said, "Yes, you really messed that one up. We wanted competition, and we could have given you a number of areas which would have worked very well. But you decided on mainframe and we had twenty years of lead time." As I discovered in a hundred ways, that story was a paradigm of RCA's problem. With the retirement of its deeply imaginative founder the company lost its thinking center in the pursuit of faddish and uncoordinated enterprises.

The programs I inherited were a microcosm of the larger company; by stretching a point one could call them educational, but they had no coherence, no common core. I tried, but in truth there was not a winner among them; the group continued, in a dysfunctional way, but I was given a further assignment in the human relations side of the company. Meanwhile I added on my own initiative a whole new dimension to my work, and I did it in a way which did not make those around me comfortable. RCA had more than its share of rigidity to go with the acquisitions, and my new venture had some gipsy elements in it.

As so often, that new road opened up innocently enough; it was the second turning that did the mischief. I had been asked to visit some AID programs in Turkish universities, and when my friend David Lilienthal heard about the trip he asked if a further leg could be added. "It's only eight hundred miles further on, and you can see what I've been doing in Iran for the last fifteen years." This *what* turned out to be a full-fledged adaptation of his TVA achievement to meet Iranian needs and conditions. He created in the south a combination of flood control, power generation and irrigated agriculture on a large scale. The first of three proposed projects was nearing completion when I got there in the winter of 1970: a sixty kilometer lake six hundred feet deep, a high dam across which I drove with the project manager (who was putting this tenderfoot through his paces); and a power line from Teheran just coming over the cliffs eighteen hundred feet over our heads. The sight of a tiny beetle attached to a thread brought the manager to confess his terror at the thought of a man riding over the abyss on a single wire to start connecting the three great turbines at the bottom of the gorge. I had seen a few remarkable places, but never anything like this, with all its promise for the country.

And there was a university. Jondi Shapur had been founded about 250 AD by Shapur II; he had done quite a bit of conquering to the westward, and he was particularly impressed by the faculty of the medical and scientific center in Antioch. "I'll build you a real university," he said, and laid out a checkerboard town just south of the future site of the great dam. (I could still see from the air the dark imprint of its streets on the light semi-desert soil.) A new institution with the old name was under construction some fifty miles away in Ahwaz, the capital of the province. At the moment I thought far less about it than I did about the five-kilometer road cut inside the mountain down to the great generators at the foot of the gorge. The parts of these had come down the

8% grade of that road at night; if the brakes failed, the driver was told to jump—fast—and let the truck break through the canyon wall without him. Both of these new encounters were fascinating, but the generators were at the moment more significant in my eyes than the university.

I went back to Teheran for a meeting with the former governor of the Khuzestan province, who had worked intimately with Lilienthal on the great project; back to Turkey for an AID university visit, and then home.

I was surprised to hear from Lilienthal again a few weeks later. Could I return to Iran at some point—soon—to look further at the university and consider organizing an advisory committee for it? The innocent 'Yes' that I gave him was prelude to an exciting mélange of experiences, from the trivial to the revealing and deeply significant. The request to accept the suggestion was met by RCA New York with amused indifference, and by the old-line company secretaries assigned to me with a fair amount of suspicion. To them it was definitely outside the company orbit.

I would soon have a plan that satisfied me but gave me an even more dubious corporate character. I stepped away from my fuzzy basic mandate in education and came back from Iran with a proposal for a subsidiary RCA marketing company. During my conversations about Jondi Shapur University I had asked several senior people about various needs which Iran might have. Their responses very quickly led to a dual suggestion: first, the subsidiary and second, a counterpart Iranian company. The latter would have a member of the royal family as a silent partner, and the dual company would deal with the legitimate needs in Iran which RCA might be able to meet.

I would find myself inhabiting some complex political and ethical issues during my eight-year association with Iran, but from the start I realized that it was only fair to apply different standards of judgment about this effort than I was used to. I learned obvious but complex lessons, above all that people could be honest in dealing with a common project, and at the same time bring widely differing social and economic assumptions to it. I had learned a good deal about this conflict within my own culture during the stress-time of the 1960s; now I would learn it in a totally new way.

I had in fact a remarkable case study in complex morality before me; and I was part of it. My judgments of financial gain and its rules had been until now truly simple. I did not even recognize the real estate opportunities that were offered me at Duke, and I would have felt them clearly a conflict of interest if I had understood them. I could be subtle in many matters, but not in these. Now I found that some of those for whom I worked in Iran stood to gain personally and substantially from programs designed for the public benefit. To complicate the matter further, those same people had risked a great deal to change the country's social fabric in many ways which I regarded as essential and valuable for its future. It was necessary for me to accept both parts of the ethical equation; neither would work without the other. I was involved in the process, but not in the equation. In other words, I was paid moderately to help things happen, but I was never a buccaneer like a good many of the non-Iranians who were swarming through Teheran at the time. (As I gradually discovered, the very simplicity of my undertakings seemed quite incredible even to my own embassy, which was used to discovering that most of its citizens were, in one way or another, a bit different and considerably more venal than they claimed to be.)

My connections, as they developed, gradually allowed me a sense of the flow of action in Iran which I would not normally have gotten. In these critical years there was a crazy logic to it all; my involvement with Jondi Shapur University came about through my friendship with David Lilienthal; David brought me the friendship of a remarkable public servant—former Director of the water and hydro project on the Iranian side and also Governor of the Khuzestan province. This new friend, Abdul Reza Ansari, had recently been without portfolio for the most honorable of reasons. He had done his many jobs too well, and inevitably he had stirred the fear and envy of some very highly placed people. Just before I came on the scene, however, he became involved in quite another arena, one that took him out of the direct line of power but gave him unique access in many ways. He was now the Chef du Cabinet for the twin sister of the Shah, who had major responsibilities in the sectors of education and the social services. In other words, all these varied activities came together, so that it seemed completely logical to develop with Ansari the idea of dual companies, and equally so that the princess should be a silent partner in the enterprise.

I shuttled back and forth like a passenger pigeon creating RCA Iran, which made up (in my eyes) for the motley set of projects my staff group was carrying on. (If my own personal need for some security had not been so great I might have heeded the advice of my superior and wiped out the whole group.) The projects at RCA, as I soon discovered, had no coherence, no common thread; they had been drawn together from various divisions where they did not fit at all, and they really cried out for a critical eye and some tough decisions. I never felt that I had a right to be high-handed with men and women who in many cases had been at RCA for years, but I did not know how to breathe life into their scattered little projects. I seized on RCA Iran with a good deal of avidity, because it gave me the freedom to try to draw ideas from the big RCA divisions. At the same time I allowed myself to be drawn into certain contentious issues such as the proper place of women and minorities in the overall structure of the company. I had a responsibility to the RCA president in these matters, but the senior men in personnel and public relations were violently opposed to raising such issues at all, and expressed their resentment to me since they could not directly oppose the president. There were other interesting issues which I raised, but it was clear that there was no real desire to have an educational component or division; it was a mismatch, and so was I. As the corporate secretary said to me, "Every time we hear you coming down the hall we say, 'Here comes Doug and he has another new idea.' You know, we don't want new ideas in RCA." As the immediate future of the company showed, this was an accurate statement—which left Iran as my primary concern.

I settled into a routine of six or seven Iran visits a year; the illusion of significance created by all this travel was in part a mask for my own continuing inner turmoil, and in part an honest self-deception. I carried on routines that had been familiar for years, but I would later see that they had little meaning. I was groping to define a space, and the glitz and glitter took over from the real significance—or potential significance—of what I was doing.

Glitz there was in plenty; once I indicated that I didn't need the sacred 53rd floor of the RCA building, I was offered a variety of spaces and wound up in the suite recently vacated by the chairman of another major corporation. Foolish, I would later say, even to notice these things; but like the Teheran apartment, the upscale travel, the new committees, the whole weary list that actually weaves a myth of importance, all of it filled a major need. The institutions I served had always lent me a major part of the meaning in my life. I gave the best of myself without reservations or compromises, and it would take me some years to find such commitment again. Certainly RCA did not invite it.

This living relationship of individual and institution had been an integral part of the college and university world for me. My job was never merely that; from the time I started to teach at Yale until I left Duke I had tried to act out my conviction that the place where I worked was alive, organic, and that I had a mandate to care for it, nurture it, encourage its growth in every way. I never learned any other way of relating to it; I neglected my family for it, I spent more energy than I had available in its service, and I was absolutely shaken when I was forced to leave.

Certainly there was enough going in Iran to distract me. The imperial family had decided to celebrate its own brief history by tying it intimately to the whole twenty-five hundred year saga of Persian royal splendor. Of course that saga was anything but consistent or even coherent, but the days of early splendor were worth summoning up, and a great party was planned at Persepolis. There were sixty-seven heads of state present, which in itself created several major problems. Among them the matter of security loomed large, and my friend Ansari (who had been deputed to organize the whole adventure) asked for RCA's help in creating a system. This was done, and a security ring surrounded the whole encampment in which each senior delegate had a great tent as his home away from home. Within this security ring everyone could move at ease, since he or she had already been thoroughly identified; but the ring was completely solid.

It truly was a spectacle, very well orchestrated and with beautiful surfaces. I was in and out of the whole show—so much so that I saw all that was painted and papered over for the occasion;

I felt however that it was a serious attempt to present the country in its best light and not, as some critics claimed, a mere exercise in ego for the Shah. There were several major books to commemorate the event, among them a fine volume of miniatures and a unique collection of archaeological and topographical charts. There was a good deal of show, but nothing shoddy. And there were, of course, humorous aspects of the affair. Given the number of small countries that sent their heads of state, the problems of protocol could become quite acute. Each was met at the airport with much fanfare, but it was often impossible to find the appropriate national anthem. As a result a generic piece was developed which could adorn many occasions—hello, goodbye, and anything in between. The goodbyes became a thorny part of the aftermath; several of the heads of state were having a far better time in Iran than they had been having at home, and they exploited the wonderful hospitality of their hosts quite shamelessly.

I had an opportunity to test the security network at the Teheran headquarters of the festival, which in less stirring times was the Hilton Hotel. I moved there from my apartment for the duration, and one evening left by car for dinner with friends a mile or so up the hill. The protocol was for the driver to return, but communication failed, and I discovered that I was beyond the outer gate of my friend's house and waiting for a car that never came. It was a fine evening, and I marched gaily down the long slope, turned to go up a small rise with the hotel at its top, and found that—for the first time in my life—I was looking, not so much at the soldier but at the automatic rifle, which barred my way. When I offered up the usual "What is all this?" routine, a very cold-eyed major in a small tent gave me two words. "Stand there." I explained that I belonged up at the hotel, had been brought through the security ring in an official car, and yes, had my business card with me. The major rubbed a finger over the engraved surface and said, "I will call." After two or three minutes of chat he relaxed a very small amount. "It seems that you exist." (But he sounded quite disappointed at the fact.) "This man will take you up." A young soldier pranced ahead up the hill and delivered me into the hands of a tall, assured man in a plain dark suit. "Dr. Knight, why no pass?" I explained who had brought me, the

Princess' private secretary; I did not know that there were passes. The dark man took a small plaque from the lapel of his jacket. "Here; put this on and you will be safe." Later on a friend looked at it and said, "I guess so." The little plaque said simply, "Imperial Guard."

But all was not fun and games. A major communications project surfaced, financed by the Canadian government through a large loan. There was a fee for placing this piece of Canadian business (the materials and labor for the project were to be largely Canadian) and that fee in turn was of great interest to two members of the royal family. One was my silent partner, but I found myself suddenly in a situation that was anything but silent. To add to the complexity of things, RCA U.S. felt that it should be the prime bidder rather than RCA Canada—a source of real conflict at home.

This mix of motives provided enough animosity for a soap opera. The clash of relatives finally had to be settled by the Shah; the corporate struggle bruised several careers; and the political fallout led to the early retirement of the Canadian ambassador. I had, at the conclusion, to endure a rebuke by the Iranian chief of military procurement. This last was a most remarkable charade; I was instructed that I must behave with strict correctness, no matter what was said or how distorted the supposed facts were. Afterward I was commended for my performance; much face had been saved, while I was made to realize that I had no face at all to worry about.

Meanwhile the situation in the country was about to take a critical turn. The 1974 increase in the price of oil affected all of the industrial nations as well as the big producers, but in Iran's case it led to major policy decisions, which in a few years would reshape the country—though not in the ways hoped and planned. Many forces were at work, but dominant were the secular and western-oriented culture of many in the controlling groups, and the failing health of the Shah. These driving forces would be countered and exploited by a radical reassertion of Islam, which was seriously underestimated by Iran's rulers and widely misunderstood in the west. I was of course affected; more to the point, I was given a second graduate course in real politics to match the

Vietnam ordeal.

The Shah's father had set the secular state in motion, but the unique geography of Iran confirmed it. The cold war and the American reestablishment of the young Shah after a major coup attempt gave the United States a heavy presence and of course allowed people like me to be invited as advisors. Dislike of this development was substantial, though in true Iranian fashion it was largely masked. The Francophile upper class culture was alienated from its own roots, the mullahs were plotting their revenge, and a group of radical students were being educated in the west. All of these conditions were dangerous but ignored.

Enter now the two overriding forces, money and mortality. The Shah knew the nature of his illness at some point in the mid 1970s, and this recognition was close in time to the radical increase of oil prices. Among his many honorable impulses was a desire to see his country in a thoroughly enhanced position before his death, which he knew must come within six or eight years. Under such pressure he began to dream of great navies and world-renowned libraries—a remarkable range of projects which (in the attempt to execute them) laid Iran open to rampant inflation and venal exploitation at every level. These mistakes in turn led to the social unrest, which gave the orthodox clerics their great opportunity. If this sounds like something out of a case study, it was. The rush of money, which was to do so much good, to add such glory to the throne and the country, was poured directly into the economy; country folk moved toward Teheran and the other major cities looking for work at high wages. They found it; wages tripled within eighteen months but productivity did not. The resulting economic pressure created exactly the unrest the clerics had been waiting for. The agitator Khomeini had been perched on the border of Iraq for fourteen years, pouring out his aggressive propaganda until it got too disturbing even for the Iran-allied sectarians in the southern corner of Iraq, and Khomeini was sent off to France. The damage had been done, however, and to the Shiite Iraquis as well. Saddam Hussein would massacre them in the 1990s with evident delight.

This antagonism between the two countries had been alive for at least eight hundred years, and it took some curious forms during my time in Iran. The general pressure which the government conveyed in all its affairs, seemed to heighten many personal attitudes and experiences. One evening I was flying down to Abadan on university business. The Iranian acquaintance sitting beside me became quite disturbed as the flight neared its end and suddenly burst out, "We're going to be over Iraqi territory for the next forty-five seconds, and those crazies down there could shoot anything and everything at us." My host, the general manager of the huge oil refinery, said much the same thing; his house on the Euphrates River was highly vulnerable, and he did not look at all cheerful as we discussed the likelihood that he might be kidnapped some dark night. "The plant will run just as well without me, but the Iraqis may not know that."

My relation to the university became 'curiouser and curiouser' over these years, and I finally came to realize how unwanted I was. This was in good part the result of fear on the Chancellor's part; everyone was watching his neighbor, and I saw that I was in an ideal position to be targeted as a spy. Beyond that there lay the resistance of French-educated administrators to the spectre of U.S. hegemony in the educational area as in so many others. Finally, there turned out to be a strong desire for some kind of public display by the committee I had assembled. The problem with them (which I could never fully explain to my Iranian friends) was their distinction. What was wanted (as I gradually realized) was a group which would have some glitter, coupled to a willingness to be feted, photographed and generally paraded around. The group I put together consisted of working stiffs, with advice to give but no spare hours for pomp and ceremony. They were too good to be decorative. (Among them were James Killian of MIT, Meredith Wilson of the Federal Reserve and the University of Oregon, and John Caldwell of North Carolina State.)

I was able to work effectively on the design of a new library— a much less threatening venture than anything involving curriculum or personnel. I came to see, however, that there was a good deal of impudence in the whole idea of transplanting my experience at any useful level. I did not have access to any real knowledge of what these students were, what they needed, what they hoped for. Jondi Shapur may have been eighteen hundred years old, but it was in a rudimentary state of redevelopment and would have to want to establish a direction for itself. This was certainly not clear to me, and I realized that the political games were increasingly important, the educational ones less and less so.

As part of the library development I tried to develop a basic book collection for an undergraduate library, tempering it to what I assumed—had to assume—were a few of the working goals and boundaries. Then I ran across the collection in literature, which was heavily into the major scholarly material in certain fields. Since one of these was my own Augustan Age (the early 18th century) I was more than curious. I didn't believe what I saw until I met the very superior and suspicious Princeton Ph.D. who clearly did not want me looking into these matters. The library had an open account with Blackwell's; the purchases were very largely directed to the interests of the few faculty who chose to follow them in some depth. Like so much else going on in Iran at the time, the library was specialized in a highly sporadic way, but with no understructure suitable for its purposes as the service university for the oil and (potentially) agriculture-rich Khuzestan province. Like a Potemkin village—or Teheran at the time of the great celebration—it had a façade of meaning with nothing inside. For many years I felt a great heaviness of heart that I had been unable to help give the university some real integrity, some sense of itself not based on my attitudes or on its external political demands but on its inner educational convictions. In this as in so much else during these years I failed. I dimly sensed the rising tension in the country and my increasingly irrelevant position there—even though I did not close my apartment until the beginning of 1978, just a few months before the final departure of the Shah.

It was only as I reflected on these years from the safe vantage point of the early 90s that I realized how pervasive was the element of incompleteness, of plans and public postures gone awry through the whole period, and how intricately connected its many manifestations were. The decade had as marked a character as that of the 60s, while its texture and tempo could not have been more alien.

Strangely enough, while this was true of the Iran I have just described—and the cause of my great frustration there—it was equally the situation here at home. The time was one of bewilderment, of deep moral searching which led to the forced retirement of a President, to the shameful vilification of our own armed forces who were guilty only of doing the things they were asked to do, and to the stagnations of a "low, dishonest decade" as Auden had already described the 1930s. The aftermath of the Vietnam War forced on us the necessity to see ourselves in new ways, and we were not yet ready to do so.

My own life was—though I did not have the insight to see it—a tiny parable of these large events of the decade. I had to confront a new structure—or rather a confluence of structures—now that my life had to be lived outside the stabilizing traditions and support systems of the university world. Since I had lived within it for so long I was unprepared for the shock of separation, for the sense of exile on the one hand and on the other the urgent need to develop some significant new career.

There were amusing aspects to this radical transition; at least they would have been so if my years of life in the president's job had not fitted me so badly to be absorbed into the bureaucracy of a giant corporation, which was, come to think of it, having its own major struggles of self-discovery and definition. As one cynical new friend (new to me but old to RCA) put it over lunch one day, "Just go quietly along and no one will notice for seven or eight years what you're doing—or not." But that did not sit well with me, and I was a maverick, too, in my lack of care about protecting myself from the normal corporate games. I was used to being exposed and alone; I was not good at walking the back pathways of power.

I was, then, ill suited to that world, while that world turned out to be baffled about itself. RCA had a remarkably coherent sense of purpose in the 1930s and 40s, which stemmed directly from David Sarnoff's vision of an integrated company which could combine the many possibilities he envisioned for radio—the equipment, the stations to radiocast it, and the programs to bring it to life. That idea was brilliantly realized in both radio and TV, but the acquisitions mania of the 1960s blurred, confused and ultimately destroyed its focus. I came into this setting, with all its outer glitz, looking for a focus to my own life and discovering all too soon that a corporate structure and a university community were very different parts of the forest. (This seemed almost too obvious a point at the time, but it would come to be a vital issue for me in the 1990s, when the corporate world had blurred the university's sense of itself.) Added to the mix, and strengthening its confusion, was my effort to make sense out of Iran even as the country fell apart.

The attempt to relate all these issues in a creative way was, I gradually realized, a magician's game, more and more clearly related to the glamorous mechanisms of my life, and less and less to any ongoing coherent experience. I found myself in a state of physical and emotional stretch between Iran and the United States, between the trip I had just completed and the one I was already planning. I had a good deal of work to do at home, but it all seemed subordinate to the rhythms of my multinational schedule. The scale of reality was skewed to this wandering life, and the mechanism became the meaning—a twist on Marshall McLuhan's famous dictum, but with the same end in view. The substance of discourse was being devoured by the rhetoric; like the pretensions of the Shah, and the lumbering misdirections of RCA, the forms of my life far transcended its inner significance. I had not, in short, found a solution to the loss of that institutional service, which had given me my order, my structure, and my assurance about my own worth.

But what about that university world at which I now looked from a distance, with an uncomfortable mingling of emotions— relief, envy, nostalgia—which was so constant a stance during these years? I continued to accept the fact that I could not return to its shelter—a shelter which was itself becoming alien to me in the painful aftermath of the sixties. There had been in that decade a crazy kind of goodness, of devotion to naïve and simple-minded ideas of redemption—the sort of insight which the synthetic folk-musical "Hair" embodied so perfectly. The terrible events of Wisconsin and Kent State shattered those fantasies; seeing Kent State from the distance of Teheran and the International Herald Tribune I thought that a great deal more than fantasy had been blown to blood and dust; I almost came home that day in order to share in the disaster—as though I still belonged to that once familiar world and its anguished time.

The real troubles in the university world turned out to be less dramatic and far more permanent than the lurid moments. The regents and trustees who deplored the sixties so vehemently had several solutions, and one was to urge the universities toward that corporate structure they themselves knew best. As a result, I found in the mid-seventies that I was doing consulting work not only with Presidents and Chancellors but with Associate Vice Provosts—a whole chain of command that had the wonderful effect of diffusing responsibility through the organization so that no one seemed to have a real grip on any given problem. I marveled at the new structures, was troubled but did not at the moment see clearly their implications and their power to distort university life. (The forces for change were so great, in fact, that they were not yet visible in their true form; we walk by a great river and have no real sense of its scope and majesty. Only the perspective of flight gives that view to us, and in the nineties I would come finally to have some of that overview.)

In the seventies I had an encounter, however, which would contribute a good deal to that later understanding. A long-time friend, now the new President of The University of Louisville, invited me to serve as a roving consultant on a part-time basis. The timing was ideal; the RCA years had ended in a similar request from the company for part of my time, and Iran was getting the rest. I had not yet rediscovered myself, but I had at least found what I did not want. It was good to be moving away from a behemoth which wanted my credentials but not my competence. Consulting would turn out to be a tantalizing, appealing though imperfect place to rest for a while.

It was both stimulating and troublesome to be close to the operation of a university again, while the place itself was so different from anything I had intimate knowledge of that I could tolerate—even enjoy—the association with all its problems. Louisville was one of the major urban public universities of the country; it came second to the state university in prestige and funding, but it was remarkable in the loyalty it commanded and the range of educational tasks it set out to perform. This was a major lesson for me; unlike the private world I knew. The public universities could have mandates laid on them which did not mesh with the main direction of the place but were regarded as essential by a ruling oligarchy. These compromises ran through the whole university; I once questioned an expenditure for the new library only to be told that, "We don't touch that item in the budget; it's the property of the political party in power."

The many demands, which often confused the central mission of the university, also accounted in part for its heavy proliferation of administrators. As I have suggested, the table of organization, with its parade of associate-vice provosts and assistants to the Executive vice president, was a massive but doomed effort to make sense of it all by linking the titles even though the functions never matched. They reflected a discomfort in the university, which (as I saw it) mirrored that larger discomfort I was coming to see in my other lives, both at home and abroad. Certainly I was being exposed (as in Iran) to one more Potemkin village of pretense; certainly the cumbersome organization was a reminder of the RCA corridors; certainly my hours of meeting with defensive or bellicose academic administrators reminded me of the doomed effort to create a coherent educational program for RCA. But there was one central difference from all my other experiences in the early seventies. The discontent and uncertainty at Louisville were real, but so were the genuine purposes and the recognition of a deeply felt need in the community. I felt that these years of encounter extended greatly my understanding of this new educational arena. Perhaps my chief value as a consultant was a result of this growth in my own insight—not an adequate sense of what my role might be, but at least one which helped make the dark, incomplete and somehow unfinished world of the seventies seem purposeful. At least my friends at Louisville told me that the discussion of their problems seemed to clarify them, and assist in major decision.

I was, however, about to find a totally new way of engaging my professional world. More accurately, and as so often before, that world came to me in a totally unexpected form—and an absorbing one. The years between 1969 and 1975 had been not only disrupted and fragmentary in many ways, but also crowded with remarkable experiences, which gave that brief period a sense of extended time and remarkably deep encounters. But none of them could have suggested the one that emerged—much too improbable to be anything but fated. I had broadened the base of my consulting work with Iran and the University of Louisville; now I was asked to give some thought to the educational marketing of a remarkable optical instrument—a telescope of such innovative design and superb finish that it could give results thought possible until now only by the use of large and cumbersome instruments. The widow of the inventor was operating the tiny company, and I had been suggested to her by intimate shared friends. We started to work together on the rather vexing educational market problems that grew from the cost of a Questar—about $2,500 in 1975, a modest price for a custom instrument but high for the average secondary school budget. The analysis was going well, I thought, and then one day my "employer" broke the mould of my professional life. "I've been President of this place for ten years, ever since my husband died. Will you consider doing it for me?" The question took me completely by surprise, and the suddenness of my answer startled me even more. "Yes, I will, if you'll stay as Chairman. You know everything about the company, and I know next to nothing." This was certainly one of the most complex decisions I had ever made, and I trusted it, though it would take me some weeks to begin to see why it was a sound idea (so far as we can ever analyze the sudden opening of a door and the walking through it to a whole new landscape). I had, in a moment's decision and without hesitation, reshaped and newly directed my life. And until I said, "Yes, yes, I will," I had not recognized how profoundly I needed such an affirmation. It was liberation after a dark six years; it was a refocusing of life after a period when my world expressed itself only in appearances, surfaces and styles. I was finally coming to terms with all that I had learned from the encounters of that time; now I was expressing the greatest of those lessons in my eagerness to step away not only from the foolish glitter of those few years, but from the many years of authority, ceremony and high public presence which had preceded them.

As I saw it—or came gradually to see it—there were many elements in this newly found order; some reached back into my early life, some were intimately tied to long-lasting intellectual interests, and some seemed to suggest a world of excitement quite different from anything I had known until now. Here was a tiny world—virtually a cottage industry—with a product of unique reputation, and one that was unique in several of the sciences. I found myself reaching back to a time when I had fancied myself a budding field naturalist/photographer. And that romantic memory was all the more compelling, since I had gone so far from it in my professional disciplines. Now the road not taken looked better than ever. The optical aspects of the Questar were remarkable. I had my first microscope when I was ten, and a cheap camera not long after. Here were the shapes of that innocent time, but as full realization of what I had glimpsed as a boy. Then I had treated these matters and interests as a dilettante who imagines himself a serious practitioner, now I could be immersed in the real thing at the highest level of quality. Above that, I saw my path leading again to a way of life I could accept fully and enthusiastically. I knew instantly and totally that the enterprise was worth it; I had not been able to say that since my exile began in 1969. If one could invent an enterprise that would be both new and yet filled with the echoes of a world long past, this Questar adventure was it. The liberation which it brought to my intellectual life was one of the most surprising by-products of the new commitment, and out of that would come a major book—major for me, at least—dealing with the turbulent sixties. Most surprising of all, there would be the chance of some imaginative work in the newest area of enthusiasm.

The decade came alive for me, of course, through the filter that I brought to it from the 60s. There was a grim sympathy in seeing the play through to its end, and to watch a whole generation of young Vietnam veterans become scapegoats as I had been. This sounds unfeeling, but it is really the opposite; certainly I did not see the full reality of the drug curse which would augment the more juvenile drugginess of the late 60s, but I saw the terrible irony of scorning the draft avoiders only to reject in the most callous way those who had been the straight arrows. If the 70s were a dark time for me, I had the company of all those who had done their duty and warped their lives. It is no accident that the Vietnam memorial is black; we lost in these years the last light of our self-confidence about just wars which had sustained us so well thirty years earlier. Even more ironically, the war that we undertook in the late 90s would be dark by definition—against terrorism but also against an attitude of intolerance, fanaticism and blackness of spirit alive in our own culture as well as that of our enemies. If the 70s gave pause to the hope of automatic social progress, the 90s would bring it to a full stop. It would be replaced by unparalleled technologic advances, which were marketed as though they mirrored and conveyed progress of the spirit, but in the darkness of the 70s we already saw the truth. My own slight, brief darkness of the spirit would turn out to be far slighter and briefer than that which affected us in the total culture.

It would be too simple—and yet not false—to say that much of the conventionality of the 70s was a first reaction to this darkness. Just as the universities turned to over-administration as a way of demonstrating that they were firmly in order again—in control of their own destinies—so the society as a whole, after surviving a true breach of law and order on the part of the President, created for itself a dullness of attitude and action wrapped in the cloak of stability. We were all busy asserting it, while we averted our eyes from our new realities of outlook and action.

SURPRISE

Demanding, not easily contained
By normal phrase or passion
Each moment lives a cube of time,
Not passive, but encountered,
Each simple phrase or leaf electric,
Heightened to counteract the waste of flesh,
Frailty of incidental powers, leaving
Us free to taste the essence,
A feast of high encounters.
The energy of age is a new world,
We live by these, each venture
Final as day's end, fresh as dawn.

CHAPTER SIX:
A New Season
1976–1989

The changes in national attitude during

the late 1970s and 1980s paralleled to a surprising degree my own recovery. President Carter may have realized his true greatness only as a retired President, but he helped the country change its tone from sourness and confusion to some renewal of order and hope. We made fun of his piety and simplicity, choosing to forget that he was a nuclear engineer and naval officer. We brushed aside the dramatic change from the seamy days of Nixon and his book-writing cronies—so trivial and yet so massive in their ethical impact. (Nothing would equal it for spectacle and social sleaze until the Simpson murders and, of course, the Clinton-Starr battle.)

Curiously enough, the President who succeeded Mr. Carter, and differed from him in so many ways, shared with him a simplistic view of the great world served by the Presidency; and they shared also a philosophic and activist pattern dependent on a few basic and deeply held beliefs. I understood these developments in the country, but did not take them with great seriousness. Looking back I realize that the demands of my tiny new world made the larger ventures of the period seem grotesquely out of human scale and purpose. Meanwhile the very element of surprise was good for me; that an enterprise so unexpected, so curious, should move into the center of my world was an occasion for wonder and rejoicing.

The company was tiny, but it made unique instruments. When I arrived on the scene the dominant one was a highly portable telescope of extreme quality—so extreme, indeed, that its performance was not believed. This was particularly true in 1950 when the prototypes first appeared, but that attitude of doubt persisted. The inventor was a gifted commercial artist with extensive technical knowledge and virtuosity; the Questar telescope was his great work of craft and art. It won major prizes for innovative design and found several unique niche markets in fields as diverse as surveillance and birding, but the astronomical market was at its center. There was more to my enthusiasm, however, than a simple desire for what W. H. Auden so wonderfully describes as "new styles of architecture, a change of heart." In part I was breathing life into a memory—the innocent excitement of those childhood days I have mentioned, with a microscope and a simple camera. The renewal of innocence in my active new life was intense and it persisted through the inevitable disappointments and missteps of my new calling.

And there was the uniqueness of the two principals in the company—both of them characters so strongly marked that it was exciting to be with them. Though Larry Braymer was a memory, he became more real than many of my flesh and blood associates. His dedication to the new instrument was constant and intense for the eight years it took to perfect the first telescope—as he said with immodest accuracy, "the first advance in telescope making for at least two hundred years." And who would not want to be in the company of a painter (superb draftsman) who could lecture Alcoa for stopping the production of a particular alloy he needed, persuade a hard-boiled patent attorney to take his fee in the stock of a company that didn't yet exist, and finally quiz each customer to see if he deserved to have a Questar? This was company heady enough to make most university professors pale by contrast.

And Peg Braymer, his wife, was just as striking. She transmitted the legend of Larry to me, of course, but it was she who commanded my attention as few others had done. Denied the education that would have made her a formidable lawyer, she took herself through a conflicted first marriage, into a magazine editorship and the support of Larry during the lean years of designing and selling the first instruments. We became intimate friends in the twenty years before her death in 1996; we had similar tastes in music and politics, we both wanted libraries (and so we founded one), we worked in harmony even when my decisions were dubious, and we had a ball doing it. My intuition and response to her first questions were wonderfully borne out.

The growth of real self-understanding in this new world would of course take the next twenty-five years of my life. Like a photographic plate the image came to me gradually, even though the decision was so immediate and confident. As I have said, I was aware of the usual exit paths for university presidents—a foundation, a government post, or a sinecure organization headship. But I was forty-nine years old when exile closed in, and I found none of the standard alternates attractive— or even feasible. Here again it took me some years to understand the nausea that swept over me at the thought of one more Board of Trustees, with its partial knowledge and self-satisfied stance. I knew that I was indicting myself, since I had accepted Board memberships that I had no time to serve responsibly; I needed freedom from these, however, as much as from my establishment career. (I was able later to smile at this reversion to my eccentric youth, but that fact did nothing to refute the wisdom of the step I took.)

My attitude at this critical moment may seem a classic case of burnout, but it turned out to have dimensions that the normal exhaustion syndrome does not show. It was positive rather than negative, a voyage of discovery rather than a trip to the breakup yard. The very diversity of my new work gave me a world to inhabit—a world as spacious in one way as it was minute in the other. Questar was and is a micro example of a 'vertical' compa-

ny, one which does its own manufacturing, marketing, development, advertising and all the rest. As if this were not enough to
set the enterprise apart, its products are un-American—permanent and created as heirlooms to be handed down from one generation to another. (This paradoxical ruggedness of sensitive
instruments means among other things that customers like the
Navy or the F.B.I. could count on restoring their much-used surveillance Questars to nearly new condition.) All of this entranced
me; unlike the passing fancies of life, it would still engage me years
later, even in a time of trouble when it should have seemed an
albatross around the neck.

There was a long-forgotten innocence about the first year in
particular, a sense almost of childlike fun in the human and technical encounters. I would come to see that these often pointed me
toward large and vexing issues; but even so they had a bright core
of pure amazement. Two would stay with me for the rest of my
life. The first was an encounter with age, the second with youth;
and both were wildly improbable.

I looked out from the bow window of my office one morning to see a stiff, overweight and clearly uncomfortable couple
haul themselves out of their car. Slowly they carried a case con-
taining a Questar into the shop. "Ah," I thought, "they can no
longer use it and want us to sell it for them." Forty-five minutes
later I saw them head back to their car, case still in hand. "Wasn't
the price right?" I asked the sales manager. "Price? No question
of that. They simply wanted to change the tracking motor in the
base. They're just back from an eclipse in Africa, and they're headed for the next in the Australian outback, where they'll want the
telescope to rotate in the opposite direction." I looked out at the
empty parking lot, trying to picture the stamina and single-heart-
edness necessary for this dedication to a remarkable subspecialty
in the world of astronomy. I realized that I was now living in a
place where astonishing people could appear in disguise at any
moment, people with none of the academic 'otherness,' the con-
trary mind that I knew so well.

My sense of this improbable world was tested quite often, but
never more spectacularly than one clear winter morning when a
wheezing VW bus disgorged a circus load of oddities. A tall, very

thin young man with peg-top jeans emerged first, followed by a young woman whose hair—vivid in that sunlight—was bright green with a Mohawk stripe of orange running from front to back. Then came three children, dirty at a distance and dramatically so close up. They wandered to the front door and into the showroom. The children meandered about, putting sticky fingers over everything. The young woman turned out to be a hopeless distraction for the sales manager because she was wearing a transparent blouse, which made her appear more naked than nudity. The young man looked all around and finally he looked at the small Questar on its tripod. "I have a hankerin' for *that*," he said abruptly, "and I want to take it with me. How much?" All common courtesy gone by now, everyone nearby was peeking through the door as he pulled out a thick roll of hundred dollar bills and peeled off the appropriate number. We have run the gamut from drug-runners to voyeur Broadway producers, but nothing has ever topped that VW bus.

My interest and creative effort were more seriously sustained by the problems to be solved and applications to be developed for our customers, who came from every federal agency, almost every state, and a great range of industries, universities and research laboratories. Our tiny company made its products in the European handcrafted way, creating permanent instruments insofar as anything fabricated and used can be called permanent. These products were uniquely valuable in certain uses and enjoyed a worldwide market as well as an impeccable reputation. Once the research vice president of a large American technical company came in order to quiet his doubts about Questar's ability to create a new kind of instrument for calibration. He asked about our customers, and I showed him a three-page list. He was clearly skeptical as he began to read; then I noticed a small quirk of the mouth turn to a large grin, and he said "Ah, the Fortune 500. Now shall we see how to meet Sperry's need?" This incident was both a celebration and a warning, like a distant lightning flash, of what it might be arrogant to attempt. I would have some major lessons in this special kind of ethical problem, although the upbeat aspects of our product and its markets were intoxicating. The daily interactions of politics, technology, profit and the developing ethos which would dominate the 80s created for me such a massive cultural change that it took me some years to see what was really going on, and the part that tiny Questar might play in the big drama.

The strange reality was that there should be such an interaction at all. Questar was in the surveillance community early because of the high portability of its lenses; combined with their unique optical quality these were non-lethal but highly effective instruments. And so I found (though the company by design had no security clearances) that I was constantly brushing against issues much in the news of the day. Far more significant, they were the issues shaping multinational relationships, particularly in Africa and the Middle East. These requests gave me insight into exotic markets, and at the same time introduced a technical problem, which would become major within ten years. This surveillance market demanded that one instrument give a broad view of a dangerous area, then a detailed image of some critical point within it. A clever design accomplished this, but within a decade the instrument was a dinosaur—the victim of bold developments in electronics and software. Suddenly we were a tiny boat running a large, extremely swift river. Could a frail company stand the constant battering of this technical shift? I was also about to experience in microcosm one of the pressures that would create the curious frenzy of the 1980s—that zeal for short-term profit, the quickly seized advantage, the fast track game. I was more than a spectator; by the end of the 80s I was an unwilling participant, drawn into ventures by my young associates, which resulted in a bitter education for us all. (In tiny scale these would parallel certain of the forced mergers of the period, and they would echo painfully the casual over-expansion of the later years, from 1985 to 1990.)

I would come to see much of this as the trendy and superficial style of the period, which had its eye on the financial manipulations but hardly at all on the products. At the time I was engaged in a venture that for the next fifteen years would add major strength to the sales picture while it compelled little interest from those around me. This was the Questar long-distance microscope, a verbal oxymoron and a major new product.

Indeed, it was more than a product. It was a new concept—but one strongly based in the optical brilliance of the telescopes. I found it to be an intellectual adventure of the first order, unlike anything I had been involved in until now. Its full nature and value were still unfolding in 2001. Quite beyond my personal excitement this new development would introduce the company to certain large, even urgent, concerns of the scientific community. The first Questars had ridden to prominence in part because of the cold war preoccupation with space. These new instruments would move toward interior space; they would press the limits of light to reveal the smallest objects and events.

Other microscopes can of course do this, but not at a significant distance from the subject. The original Questar had some of this capability almost as a by-product of its telescopic qualities. What the Questar Chairman and I did was to experiment with changes in the curves of the optic, so that the subject view was brought steadily closer until it reached a limit at 22 inches. At that distance we were able to resolve—that is, to see with complete clarity—objects as small as 2.5 microns. A few years later we were confronted by a customer with an acute need to see objects one micron in size, again at a significant distance from the target. The optics were much more complex, but the design was successful. Unlike the earlier microscope, the new one called for highly sophisticated light paths within the barrel of the instrument. The result was dazzling—one micron resolution at a distance of 15 cm. from the target

What was the unique value of this distance? A micron is a millionth of a meter—a red blood cell is 7 microns or so in size. To see this without invading the subject means that if it is alive, moving, toxic, extremely hot, under great stress, one can observe it, measure it, watch it change without risk either to the target or to the observer. The possibilities seemed almost overwhelming to us, and fifteen years later they are still so. A few have been realized, but we are still at work on uses not yet understood. (That may seem an odd statement, but I have discovered in the last twenty years that often a new instrument is well in advance of its uses. It goes to seek them, rather than the other way around.)

The world of optics is so mysterious at this frontier that the full quality of the instrument would not emerge for another ten years. I had been working on biomedical uses of the microscopes as part of my rapprochement with Duke, and in 1996 my two closest friends in the Eye Center called me urgently to come for a review visit. There on the laboratory bench was a Questar 100—the 1-micron version—but I found the eyepiece in a new position. When I looked I saw a true stereo image of the target—not the illusion of stereo given by a binocular eyepiece, but the real thing. It is a quality so remarkable that we have kept it to ourselves until now, in the summer of 2001, when we have been granted a domestic patent with foreign registrations. (I have reached ahead in time to extend the story of this instrument, because it is a remarkable example of the excitement which inhabits the Questar enterprise—remarkable for both its nova quality and its continuity with the past.)

It was in the exploration of possible uses of this new instrument that I found myself intersecting a range of scientific or technical ventures in which the Questar microscopes might play a part. I was forced to admit, however, that *might* was all too often the operative word. Many bright ideas simply did not compel enough attention from potential users to lift them above the level of curiosity; enough did, however, to keep me at it while my young colleagues in the company were chasing larger and brassier sales. I was now traveling that road not taken, the whole other side of my self that I had turned away from at the start of my Yale years. I realized that it was not an interest based on mathematics, statistical measurement or data tabulation. It was a far more primitive and exploratory interest that drove me—that child's excitement at first learning that his world has many scales, dimensions and miracles to be admired, wondered at. I did not pause for this analysis at the moment; I simply responded again as I had when I was ten and had my first glimpse of the new world through a microscope. At the same time, however, the most advanced medical possibilities continued to tantalize me. I was certain that the markets were there because I was convinced that I could show my clients some things they had not seen before. And so it came to pass, though without the immediate breakthrough to a new and larger medical market I had dreamed of.

That remark sounds as though I had succumbed to the growth mania, at least in some microscopic way. The opposite was rather the case. When my close friend the Chairman of the Duke Eye Center said, "I have seen two things in the eye that I never saw before. I theorized about them, but now I know how they actually look," I found the moment quite reward enough. What I wanted was not the large numbers, but the high respect that I felt the instruments deserved. Indeed I looked on their unique quality as an antidote to the passion for quantification, which seemed to be running through American society like a virus. The dismal phrase "bottom line" was used and misused for every situation—often as a substitute for precise thought. It became a metaphor for supposed hard-headedness, and it became also one of a group of phrases which all pointed to the positive balance sheet as the most important part of the enterprise—no matter how arrived at. The merger mania that developed during the decade seemed to be driven by this same naïve form of dollar worship; like the bank mergers just getting underway, there was a profound illusion at work. To be a capital center was an automatic "good thing."

As part of that informal graduate course in business, which was my life at the time, I had a sudden and potentially savage encounter with this mode of thought—which I had felt Questar was too small to be involved in at all. We had been doing our company banking with a staid, almost mythically proper Philadelphia bank that showed a high respect for our eccentric company. One morning the Girard Bank and Questar woke up to discover that we had been acquired by Mellon Bank, which at that moment was highly aggressive in its plans to become a major capital center. It was never to manage that, but along the way it decided that small customers were nothing but trouble-—especially small customers without deep pockets. I was summoned to a meeting in Philadelphia where a number of hatchet men discussed— over my head—how to clear-cut companies like ours in order to make room for their kind of free enterprise. "We can have someone in there by Monday to straighten up the operation," began the chief destroyer; as the discussion of the means to accomplish this went on I realized that the Questar enterprise I believed in so completely was to be dismembered and sold in order to recover the operating capital which had been lent by Girard.

It was assumed that I had nothing to say in the matter; as I remembered it later, I had to hold on to the edge of the table to give me some small sense of reality. It sounds melodramatic in retrospect, but I felt a great wave of nausea as I realized that they totally believed they could do to us whatever they wanted—and by their standards they certainly could. I stood up. "You will not put anyone in the company on Monday to wreck it. I will find money elsewhere, and I will let you know." As I went to my car I could not believe what I had done; there had been an assertiveness, a combativeness on my part that I didn't know I had—in this form, at least. Now all I had to do was to prove my point by finding the money. The Questar Chairman and I did it together; we went to an old friend, a local banker with a legendary reputation for the intuitive soundness of his loans. I would look back on this adventure as the closest brush with corporate disaster I had encountered—and disaster is an understatement.

While I was developing this whole new structure for my intellectual and active life I was sustaining my educational ties (at a suitable distance) through my work with the Woodrow Wilson Foundation. I became its Chairman in 1982, and for the next eleven years would share in its constant attempts to define its mission as the foundation world veered sharply away from the period of straight-arrow graduate fellowships. These had gone by the board when the Ford Foundation project ended, only to be replaced by the new Mellon Fellowships in the humanities. They were important and timely, but they did not speak to the range of educational issues that had become insistent in the country at large. (It was in these years, after all, that the corporate model became a truly aggressive influence in university design. Equally it was a time when the great university financial campaigns began to perpetuate themselves, when the bidding wars began to create a new generation of wandering scholars, a time when the issues of political correctness began their divisive and litigious career.)

It was heresy to my more conventional friends on the Board of Trustees, but I felt that certain small budding projects pointed the way to the solution of major issues for the country at large. The graduate fellowships addressed an elite portion of the educational community, and they tended to concentrate this selectivity even more because of the preeminent graduate schools chosen by many of the recipients. The Institutes for secondary school teachers, on the other hand, spoke to a major and broadly based problem; they were designed to bring these high school teachers together with some of the most creative faculty in the universities. The first programs were in the sciences, and they were so effective that the concept was borrowed by the National Science Foundation and substantially funded there. The Woodrow Wilson recipients were asked to replicate such programs in their own regions, and this worked so well that many thousands of teachers were reached in a ten-year period. This, I felt, was the type of program which spoke to a great need, and combined vision and practicality in meeting it.

As I have suggested, my view of other emerging patterns in higher education was by no means so assured or optimistic. In a way I regretted that my corporate experience made me so sensitive to the effort——initiated in the early 70s and more assertive each year—to impose a corporate model on the structure of university administration. There were two major dangers in this development, as I analyzed it. Many elements of rigidity and redundancy in corporate administration were beginning to clog the arteries of university life. And the style of corporate operations brought a good many unwelcome side effects. Above all it fostered a set of distortions which began to redefine the purposes of the university. I would consider all of these issues in much greater depth during the 90s, but I could already see that administrative staffs had tripled over a twenty-year period, that research was measured more by volume than by insight or creativity, and that intellectual honesty was becoming steadily degraded in a world where financial reward could so easily erode the integrity of the research being done. The very abuse of bottom line, as I have said, showed all too clearly where certain patterns of thought were headed. (Honesty of mind, after all, has nothing to do with the *bottom line;* its standards are expressed elsewhere, and in other images.)

That remark was rank heresy to the dominant voices of the 80s. Their ears were filled with other imperatives—a Secretary of the Navy who demanded a six hundred ship Navy and a compliant Secretary of Defense who allowed him to build it; a President who espoused a hard line with "the evil empire" but encouraged the worst of games to be played in Central America. These were the style-setting actors of the time; excesses were mirrored in ungoverned corporate mergers, and in a spurious prosperity whose deficits would haunt us for a decade. I looked on in horror, knowing well that in this great game my small voice and tiny enterprise made virtually no difference—but might still be caught in the dark consequences of such politics.

There was a major ethical problem here, which I first met in college, where a dozen public causes tugged at me to espouse them and take to the streets. Now, with much of a lifetime already behind me, I was asked to take a position again—and asked this time by the voices inside who told me that these national policies were wrong and destructive. I was far clearer about this than I had been fifty years earlier, and I was also far clearer about the limits on my freedom to choose than I had ever been—limits that once again showed me my lack of power to influence events. I found an answer to such ethical distortions in my power to use a totally different standard in our own effort, through the instruments our company created. This was better than protest, because something worth making was kept in place. (I would adopt much the same stance in the 1990s, planting a tree rather than cursing the timber companies, voting my conscience rather than proclaiming that the political system was hopelessly corrupt.) I was beginning to feel disillusioned with the cynics, even the cynics whose basic tenets and judgments were much like my own.

Some part of this developing serenity and inner security was generated by my discovery in the mid 80s that I could finally return to the 1960s. Just as I found that I had new and creative relationships at Duke (which in 1969 I was sure could never take place) so I found that the whole complex crisis of thought and action that made up the 60s was now the one subject I must deal with. For two years I spent the evenings reading and annotating the substantial literature that had accumulated; then one May morning (I would never forget it) I decided that I had read enough and taken enough notes. I closed the file drawer and rarely opened it again. Instead I set out to write two pages a night—in longhand, of course—and nine months later had a first draft of everything but the Duke section. This I had planned not to write, staying instead on a high and philosophic plane of discussion. The Duke Press shocked and delighted me twice, first by wanting to publish the book and then by insisting that a very personal Duke chapter had to be part of it. Of course they were right, and soon I was forced to admit it.

Somewhat to my surprise, I found that this intense work with the 1960s gave me a perspective on the 80s. Even the passionate excesses of the earlier period heightened by contrast the banality of the 80s and early 90s. George Bush's immortal allusion to "the vision thing" struck at the heart of the problem. One could certainly say that the 60s had too many visions, but in looking back as I prepared to write I was startled to find that virtually all of the causes of that period had both substance and staying power. Major problems as diverse as scientific integrity, relevant university education and racial integration in the university context were as vibrant as ever, and no closer to satisfactory solution. They were the educational version of society's larger ills, and my position outside the Academy allowed me a clear vision of the daily trouble and disruption that a failure to deal with them would cause. I was, in short, increasingly disturbed by the decade, both as it seemed to be luring Questar into some dubious design and marketing projects and as it encouraged false standards in its emerging social, ethical and intellectual life. There was indeed a transference of corrupt values among these three arenas, which was the precursor of rough times to come.

I came to see two major aspects of this unease. First, it had been a long time developing, and its roots went back to that euphoric post-war period when the world, as the techno-pundits saw it, would offer us unlimited energy to do our work, and endless leisure for our enjoyment. Now in the late 80s we had to recognize that we were working longer hours, traveling greater distances, fighting to understand the mythologies of our past and our future. The illusion of benevolent nuclear power was now unraveling in a dark way indeed. We found that we had been experimented on, that we were guinea pigs; and that we had not even designed a way to handle the inevitable waste products of our new technology. Futurist myths were just beginning to show themselves, but they were the same old ones of limitless horizons, greater ease, multiple communication. (This wedding of communication systems and computer control would in the 90s give us a whole new set of dubious assurances about our future to replace the failed old ones.)

I discovered as I was bombarded by this second wave of fabulous futurism that I could look into its heart without the constraints I would once have felt. In part this was the result of completing *Street of Dreams.* As I mastered that period to my satisfaction—well, almost—I felt detached from the glib and chic thought-patterns of the late 80s. I had come to see that many aspects of its growth were destructive and that the supposed efficiencies of size were often the opposite. It was quite clear that the fad of takeovers had benefited the lawyers and bankers but much less often the shareholders and the consumer public. Without being sentimental about smallness, I was seeing its possible economic virtues as well as those others touted by the social romantics.

As a result I found myself in a paradoxical position, serene yet aware of growing tension. My young turks were pressing hard for the big sale and rapid growth. I felt set aside by them to a considerable degree, while I had to find the capital for the new projects. In my eagerness to encourage those who were to come after me, I was being untrue to my own best thought—and judgment. The company and I would both regret it.

It was strange and disturbing that at almost every point during the decade our microscopic experiences were parallels to the huge financial events taking place around us. Our encounter with Mellon Bank was an exact parallel to the procedures of a hostile takeover, and Bill Losch the friendly banker was—again in the lingo of the moment—our white knight. Similar also was the passion of my young colleagues for rapid expansion, with unrealistic (because unquestioned) hopes for rapid growth and glittering results. This national attitude led among other major events to the mini-crash of 1987; more generally it was responsible for a years-

long preoccupation with financial manipulation but not produc-
tive innovation. These illusions took a special form at Questar; we
put capital into ideas with considerable growth possibility, and
then failed to develop the product fully or to stick to its marketing in the face of slow initial interest. We were ahead of the market with a remote measurement system, but when we found that·
hard work was needed to sell it, we turned away. This was a great
frustration to me, for the people who turned away were the very
ones who were to provide the continuity of our management. We
found ourselves as a result in several years of trouble that came
close to destroying us.

Through all this discord there were two bright and important
strands of action—the Chairmanship of the Woodrow Wilson
Foundation, and the deeper exploration of certain major scientific and medical uses of the new microscopes. The second would
be particularly valuable for my future scientific encounters, while
(as I have already indicated) Woodrow Wilson was a unique privilege in these years. I had set out after 1969 to make a new world
in full recognition of the fact that I was an exile. The ideal university as well as an idealized life within it were always alive in my
mind. While the Woodrow Wilson Foundation served various
selected sectors of the educational world it was also an epitome of
the whole, an embodiment of standards and attitudes that were
vital for me. Above all it served the world of the teacher, dearest
to me of all my careers. I suffered from the loss of it during those
dark years in the 1970s, and had been fortunate enough to find
an unusual reentry by teaching a class of my peers. The Woodrow
Wilson Chairmanship paralleled almost exactly this personal
teaching renascence, and the two taken together were an antidote
to the hard battles of the decade.

I had been a trustee of the Foundation since its formal beginning in 1957; of all the committees, consortiums and Board
memberships I had inhabited this was the one that endured. I had
once used the word *nausea* to evoke my reaction to most of them,
and by now I could see why. They made their mark by talky meetings, sometimes at fashionable watering holes like Aspen, Bellagio
or their less upscale counterparts. From the talk flowed reports,
and from the reports flowed…nothing, for the most part. By con-

trast, Woodrow Wilson had one overriding virtue; it was activist almost by definition. Often this activism was responsive; a client or a program came, and the Woodrow Wilson staff showed its quality both in developing the idea and then administering it economically and with great style. I could relate directly to this, and it was a confirmation of my commitment to a similar activist philosophy when I was asked to be Chairman.

The work of the Foundation turned out to be a commentary on the decade and in an odd way an exploration of it. There were new and financially generous programs of secondary school teaching; there were short-lived projects in which other Foundations took advantage of Woodrow Wilson by allowing it to develop programs which were then retrieved by the funding source once they had been established. It was a stimulating, restless time as these new ventures were developed and tested. There was growth that allowed good things to be done; it was exploration free of the worst qualities of the decade. It was vigorous and inventive, without the dark aggressions which marked fields like foreign policy with its Iran-Contra schemes, or the predatory business practices, and the adoption of bad corporate style by the universities. I would consider the meaning of these emergent patterns far more deeply in the coming decade; here it came to be one more aspect of a failure of leadership and a yielding to expediency, which I saw more and more clearly as the tone and style of the time. I would have to make a reckoning with it myself; my attempts to remove myself from the daily management of my tiny company showed some of the same muddled motivation that was writ large in the world around me. I had succeeded in putting my personal world back together, in part by exorcising the darkness through the writing of *Street of Dreams,* but my criticisms of the later decade demanded some resolution and if possible some transcendence in my understanding of a wise path to follow.

On reflection, the second half of the 80s seemed not only discordant but destructive. We spent ourselves into a huge deficit position so that our prosperity was an illusion. The one major gain from the money spent on military force could have been had at a fraction of the cost—as our own Intelligence groups knew very well. More dangerous for the future, however, was our lack of understanding about the end of the cold war. The major pressures of the 90s would flow directly from it; they would demand a whole new range of perception from us as the single superpower. There would be great opportunity and great danger.

My own reckoning with the discordance of the time had two major aspects, and they came to me in sequence: first, a new and deeply exciting focus for my work, and second, a fundamental shift in my view of education deriving from the major venture in self-education which my professional effort demanded. The new version of the microscope had breathtaking qualities, which defined in good part my own discipline. I had to bring myself to a point where I could do some justice to its qualities and possibilities. I have mentioned the fact that my young colleagues had dollar signs in their eyes, and that we invested heavily in systems that were never fully perfected—and which, incidentally, would make a decade of trouble for us. I was in another part of the forest; I felt committed to certain basic scientific possibilities of our new instrument. As a result I committed myself to a dual path of learning; I had to understand the instrument, and I had to learn how to persuade others to take it seriously. The original Questar had confronted this same problem; it too violated the previous conventions of instrument performance. Just as the Braymers committed themselves totally to *making* it understood, so I had to make myself understand it so that I could teach others.

A major result followed from this discipline; I began to realize that I had come full circle in my intellectual concerns. I was back to the sciences, but in a way that implied a whole new view of education—an activist view, one that involved both the act of learning and its application—its relevance, to go back to the 60s— as one complex event. This awareness developed in the context of a curiously conflicted time. The decade of the 80s was clearly one of diverse and even urgent activity—by no means wise in its use of national resources or its treatment of its weaker citizens, but full of the driving force which the 70s had so thoroughly lost. My own experience ran in parallel with this national experience at many points, but I began in addition to see another kind of growth in myself, slower and more tentative than the forces in action all around me. By the end of the decade I realized that I had undergone a major change in perception and indeed of basic attitude toward my world. The twilight sense of academic exile was changing to a dawn of education as active, an essential component in every aspect and function of my life. The liberal education I had preached for so many years had become an essential part of the creative effort I was making every day—an effort that involved equal parts of learning and public action as we presented these new instruments and their pioneering uses.

Most striking was the correspondence I found between this personal liberation and the diaspora of education through so many social structures. I was not yet fully conscious of all that this redirection would mean (that would be a major perception of the 1990s) but I could at least see clearly that the academic world and the world of active education too often traveled different roads to different ends. In the years just ahead I would find that one of my personal mandates would be an attempt to reconcile them.

------------➤ 181

BATTLES

That war I never fought stays with me,
Still muttering, like guns at night,
Distant, in the back of my skull
Where all the Japanese was to be stored,
To use for secret purposes;
But I was stranded on the battle beach.

The debt to my friends is not
To be repaid; impossible
To price their lives. They live
Forever humorous, young, incredibly
Intent on what they did. I sail
With them on those voyages
I never made and know by heart.
Their legacy to me was
A gift from gods—glorious,
Ambiguous, nearly fatal.
I moved smoothly to my calling,
Advanced with golden apples
For my toys, toys of success and pride.
But step by step the games I played
Revealed their rules. I had flown
Into a great web; it held me
Firm to its purposes—not
The intimate terror and triumph
Of my friends, but something

Insidious, a smog of anger and resentment
In which I was an appointed victim
And had the world's ugly ways
Thrust down my throat, as though
I could digest them, make them harmless.
That was bad magic, to see
And like Cassandra have no power to change
All that I hated in that decade—
Worse, be the puppet of it, not the savior.
It was a new hell—
So mixed with heaven there was no way
To sever them as they wove
One monster web, deformed
All of us who endured it.
That was a war with nothing
Honorable—but the belief in honor,
Like those who died on Okinawa beaches
And gave me the chance to fight
This second war, of cultures
And causes, where there was
No certain way but endless mazes
Of childish right and arrogant wrong:
That was my legacy from friends
Dead in far places. My unresolved battles
Confirmed their clarity,
Their single purpose, their victorious end.

CHAPTER SEVEN:
Where   We   Stand
Fall, 2001

Recent events have forced a new and
greatly enhanced context for this modest, personal book. I
have made certain claims about the ability of liberally educated people—indeed the duty—to shape the active world. Now
the word action itself has assumed a new and hideous form,
one that must be confronted not only by our physical power
but even more urgently by the inquiring, valuing minds of our
society.

That action has moved us a long step beyond any narrow
nationalism of goal and purpose. We are forced to establish our
purposes in terms of our deep convictions—our sense of what is
most valuable in our society—not merely on the easy structures of
the nation. Our enemies struck at the symbols of our nationhood
as they saw them; their view stands in almost complete opposition
however to all that we really embody and believe.

The great issues that have redefined the nation-state during
the last century are themselves issues of human awareness that

rigid nationalism could not satisfy. Our gradual move toward social structures that might be both sub-national and multi-national is the clearest form of a shift which now moves to new urgencies and sharper definitions. Along the way, the perpetual issues of disparity in wealth and status have become fully visible through the new media and the many means of world communication. Economic and social structures are also far better understood—or rather, half-understood; all of this has added to the tension that feeds the forty or fifty 'small' wars underway at any given moment. Those wars stem directly from the clash between community or tribal needs and a world order that defines and shapes the larger issues of power.

There we see a partial setting for the malignant attitudes that could shape and mature terrorist organizations. In particular we see how the full range of such conflicts is displayed in the Middle East. There it is all present, all long-standing, and all available for a leader of unusual intelligence with the power to reach very widely for his elite corps of violent followers. Together they have exploited legitimate human concerns and turned them into inhuman action. This is the great path that tyrants have always followed. There is nothing new about it except the technical brilliance of the best terrorist operatives. They have turned against us the tools that a multi-national society has created to serve its purposes; from that perspective the recent and definitive attack was a superb symbolic statement. The fact that it was also a savage anti-human act has been intensified by its success.

The extreme focus which we give that disaster, however, must not distract us from the larger, more permanent issues—issues of our understanding and action, in which the liberally educated mind has a crucial part to play. These issues have an extremely wide range: the existence of radical evil; the dilemmas of relationship between the rich and poor countries; the need to reconcile profound religious/cultural conflicts; the particular need for the United States to understand and use wisely its unique wealth, its cultural as well as military and financial power; and finally the protection and advancement of our intellectual and cultural center in the face of frontal and perhaps lengthy attacks on it, all of which we face.

Radical evil is not a comfortable reality for the educated community to face. Those of us who lived with the revelations of the Nazi regime and then the deeply violent sub-culture of the civil rights struggle do not—if we are honest with ourselves—find it hard to recognize this radical evil when it shows its face. Social scientists have tried since the 18th century to argue it away, however, and the theory of sustainable progress was one result of their analytic models. We can in any case get so involved in the causes of any great and dark event that the reality itself is obscured. In this arena the artists have understood far better than the technicians of cultural analysis where realities lie. The most 'objective' efforts at cultural deconstruction leave us with the naked reality that some men and women are evil; they damage and destroy others and ultimately the fabric of society itself. If this is not true, the Greek tragedians, Shakespeare and the great epic writers have written to no purpose, have dealt with fantasy.

Within that basic recognition of evil we can proceed to think through the issues that are so clearly defined by the current conflict. The conflict of rich and poor countries, like that of rich and poor people, is always with us. It has been heightened and greatly extended in our multi-cultural, multi-national world. One major purpose of the United Nations, after all, is to ease these deep discrepancies, while—no matter how well-intentioned we are—none of us can deny that in a world with very few financial borders or constraints wealth will flow to the most sophisticated countries. There is no need to rehearse Econ 101; the issue is one of understanding, controlling and modifying this flow-pattern so that it does not create the envious resentment that leads our enemies to turn anger into hatred for our whole culture. In extreme hands this hatred becomes a political weapon, of course, with a far different purpose than the explicit cultural attack. Power becomes the real issue—that dream of every tyrant. I maintain that if we weaken the appeal of this attitude we not only strengthen our world society but we deflect one major weapon of our implacable enemy. Our abuses of power (the colonial curse) were never adequately balanced by the intermittent rule of law. In our future we have a simple purpose which demands extremely complex means. If we reduce the inequities we all benefit; the events of September 11,

2001 and after demonstrate the truth of what I say; these inequities are a weapon against us, and we must improve on the performance of such institutions as the World Bank and the International Monetary Fund to meet valid needs without imposing standards which do not always mesh with the culture of individual societies.

Equally complex and important is the need to resolve certain worldwide tensions of spiritual and religious conviction. The subject is difficult, almost dangerous to verbalize because we live in a time of great spiritual hunger and great confusion about the means of meeting it. Our ease of communication makes it possible to sample a dozen faiths at first hand—and indeed the gurus make it easy by coming to us, first class and beautifully packaged. They give classes, they can mitigate our ailments, they assure us that it is easy to be in a state of grace—*their* state of grace. At the same time there has been a remarkable resurgence of the great traditional patterns of faith, often in a simplified—sometimes even primitive—form. To say this is not to disparage them, but we must understand that they are in part a reaction to an overly cynical approach to religious faith, and equally to the 'progressive' .forms of religion in which good works and busy communities have obscured the inner life of the spirit. This yearning for a personal encounter with the *Other,* the more than human, is expressed in all the major faiths, but it is of course most obvious in the secularized west. Many of us moved our traditional forms of faith out the front door only to have them come in through the window—old dogmas with new shapes and new urgencies.

And by an odd perversion some of the most violent political movements of our time—the most nihilistic—are fuelled by these changing shapes of faith. The Bin Laden terrorist structure has benefited from these unrooted as well as disenfranchised groups. Clearly the neo-nazi and Aryan groups have trained and encouraged people who are available as recruits for the extreme version of Islam turned loose by the Taliban and given its international cutting edge through the leadership of Bin Laden and his core group. The rich cultural soup of faiths, causes and anti-causes has become the perfect setting for a brilliant, highly coordinated small group to build its strike force. We must never forget that this central group has provided a religion for those who are desperate for one. It may be a religion whose god is the pleasure of hatred—of striking back at an enemy, any enemy—but it is still a religion. We will not be effective in our struggles for an ordered yet multiple society—of which, once again, we are the world's greatest example—until we recognize that the forces driving our antagonists are equally complex. Their systems of value are the mirror image of our own.

The burden laid on us, the citizens of the United States, is a great one. It is so not primarily because we have earned the hatred of violent people, but because such a great door has been opened for us. When the President spoke just after September 11 he said that the event was a defining moment for us, one that gave us as a country the chance to establish our place in the new century. I must give him great credit for this; it was far more searching than I expected. But that broad base of responsibility is one that we must now examine, explore in its many meanings. The current battle will be merely negative unless we can define our deepest kinds of service to this disordered world.

Our assets: we have wealth, power, culture diversity, generosity of heart, and a fuzzy but widely shared set of humane principles governing our relations with each other. Our liabilities in dealing with world issues at this new level of violence: naiveté, some serious degree of arrogance (much of it unconscious); a love of grown-up toys, often as a substitute for deeper encounters with reality; an impatience in everything we do, which leads to a passion for instant results: a tendency to believe that the good things of life are to be had by working harder, faster, more competitively than our peers in other societies.

How does this bundle of qualities play out when we are challenged so frontally? Winston Churchill had to answer that question about us at the start of the Second World War and well before we were officially involved. "My countrymen said, 'The Americans are a remote and luxurious people; they will not join us in our time of danger.' And I said, 'You do not understand the Americans; you have not studied the great Civil War.'" And Churchill went on to point out our tenacity in defending a great cause, and our power to see an issue through to its conclusion.

Churchill read us correctly; we are given to great extremes, great impetuousness, but we are at the same time unwilling to settle for half-success. This quality will be tested severely, because we are now in a conflict without glory, where cunning and tenacity must be our great weapons. Our straightforwardness, one of our major virtues, must now be subordinate to our cleverness, ingenuity and power to react quickly to attacks and affronts. The same is true for many of our other virtues; we must reshape them to the occasion, while we protect our openness of attitude and action as far as possible.

Our greatest challenge, then, in the face of these multiple attacks, which constantly turn against us our strength as an open society, will be to keep our essential character and teach ourselves to see it in new ways. We are bringing our skills in medicine and technical operations, for instance, to bear on the current problem of bio-terrorism. Beneath and beyond those steps of action lies the constant need to analyze our problems, not primarily in a technical way but in a comprehensive humane but critical way— one which allows us to hold in the mind a whole set of complex variables. As a set these are obvious (military, political, ethical, medical, each in its strategic as well as tactical character) but when we put them in motion there is nothing easy or obvious about them. Each impinges on the other. They are in motion together, a whole galaxy of options. At precisely this point the liberally educated leader has the best chance of making wise decisions. The whole thrust of his education has been a training in complexity— of attitude, decision, of the consequences of a given action. In this way his education has sensitized him to the world of choices—and that most difficult kind, which must be made without full knowledge either of the prior conditions or the future consequences. He must hold this uncertainty in mind, and then take the step of decision. The choice of moment is critical; Lincoln knew that he could not emancipate the slaves until his armies had scored a significant victory. That requirement shows us how clearly he saw the momentous nature of the decision itself; radical abolitionists would have had no hesitation and might very well have caused the permanent division of the country.

When we think of the decisions made by Lincoln or Truman,

we realize that an educated leader is not created by his cultural antecedents or his academic degrees. Both men had educated themselves, however, to weigh the full complexity of issues, and above all to estimate the balance of good and evil in situations where the evidence was blurred. At the start of the Korean War Truman was faced with a sudden massive attack. As he tells it, he asked his senior group to meet at dinner (the attack had come in the late afternoon). Then he shut the doors and turned to them. "How many hours have we?" "About five, if we want to make a significant choice." He then went around the room asking each man in turn to tell him everything he knew about the problem. Truman listened, saying very little. At 11:30 he said, "The time is up; we must move." And with that he went upstairs to bed.

The stories point to the heart of my concern with liberal learning in action. Obviously we cannot make leaders of this quality in the classroom, but we can teach something about living with complexity, with decisions that must be definitive although the evidence is not. That discipline of mind is as essential as all of the technical skills on which we must depend for the success of our society in these difficult years.

It follows, finally, that the arts and humanities, which teach us the nature and practice of that complexity, are essential, no matter what immediate demands and stresses are brought to bear on us. The experience of my life has validated this conviction, this basic judgment of value, which I have evolved over a lifetime and still try to confirm in my active life today.

Printed in the United States
1210800003B/259-306